DEMONS RULE™

TABLE OF CONTENTS

DEDICATION

I would like to thank the following individuals for assistance in playtesting and/or designing this adventure: Eric (Girder) Spahr, Steve (Cal Tensian) Adamczyk, Mia ("Why does everything always attack my Pegasus?") Tokatlian, Randy (Snake-Eyes/Uzi) Gates, Jeremy ("I think I can handle running (yet) another character...") Cash, and anyone else that I've forgotten who was involved in the playtest runs. I would also like to acknowledge my debt to the following: Kelly Blades, who made me sit through The Warriors a few years ago and thus, at least in part, inspired a major portion of the plot; H.P. Lovecraft and all who've followed in his footsteps, for providing me with the inspiration for the rest of it, and I would like to thank the principal editor of this work, Rob Bell, for helping me to realize that it is best to think things through before writing them down...

CREDITS

Author/ Designer: Charles Brown

Editors: Rob Bell & Chad Brinkley

Cover Illustration: Ted Boonthanakit

Interior Illustrations: Joven Chacon

Layouts: B.T. Thompson

Project Specific Contributions: *Series Editor:* Rob Bell; *Pagemaking, Layout, Cover Graphics:* B.T. Thompson; *Proofreading:* David Mercier.

ICE MANAGEMENT — *Art Director/Production Manager:* Terry Amthor; *Sales Manager:* Deane Begiebing; *Editing & Development Manager:* Coleman Charlton; *President:* Peter Fenlon; *CEO:* Bruce Neidlinger; *Controller:* Kurt Rasmussen.

ICE STAFF — *Marketing Consultant:* John Morgan; *Print Buyer:* Bill Downs; *Production Supervisor:* Jennifer Kleine; *Editing & Development Staff:* Terry Amthor, Kevin Barrett, Rob Bell, Pete Fenlon, Jessica Ney, John Ruemmler; *Graphics & Production Staff:* Edward Dinwiddie, William Hyde, Andrew Christensen, Brion Thompson, Eric Bruns, Kevin Williams; *Sales & Customer Service Staff:* John Brunkhart, Jo Lori Drake; Finance and Administration Staff: Chad McCully, Karl Alexander Borg; *Shipping Staff:* John Breckenridge, Kurt Fischer, David Johnson, David Mercier.

Printed in U.S.A., First Printing 1990

Produced & Distributed by Iron Crown Enterprises, Inc., the exclusive manufacturer of Hero Games.

STOCK #: 412
ISBN 1-55806-110-X

INTRODUCTION

This Adventure is intended for 2-8 *Champions* characters with Defenses between 20 and 30 and with 45-60 Active Point attacks. With minor modifications this adventure could be played by any number of characters in any point range.

Anyone planning to play in this adventure should stop reading at this point.

PROLOGUE

The chamber stands shrouded in darkness so deep that the candles, set at several points around a rune inscribed circle, provide only dim illumination. Slowly, a dull green glow begins to fill the room.

This glow originates from the gems set into the foreheads of the three figures that sit around the circle. As the glow intensifies, one of the men removes a scroll from the center of the circle and begins to read. The others repeat the incantation and rise slowly to their feet. Green light lashes out from the gemstone in the forehead of the scroll-bearer, splits into two beams above the center of the symbol, and continues on towards the gems of the other two men. Soon all three are bathed in an eerie green aura, and the chanting grows louder.

The light reveals several armed men who wait around the perimeter of the chamber, with their heads bowed either in repose or reverence.

The point where the light-beams meet begins to expand. Tension mounts in the room.

Soon it will happen!

Without warning, two of the chanting cultists collapse in pain; the light from their gems dims. The armed figures around the room jump to attention. Something is going wrong!

Suddenly, the third man screams, the green light dims, then fades completely, only to be replaced by a malevolent red glow. A faint wind stirs in the room, and a figure begins to form above the center of the diagram. From this figure comes a voice that is not of this world.

"Free, at last! You, mortal, who think yourself a wizard, you shall aid me in retaking this world. Your guards are useless, as they will suffer the same fate as your allies did!"

Looking at the smoldering skeletons of his fellow Morbanes, the man shudders. He fears that this creature is right, and that he now must do its bidding, regardless of his own desires. He also knows that now, because his DEMON Lair tried to summon and enslave a Nether Lord, his world is doomed...

GM NOTES

ADAPTING THIS ADVENTURE TO OTHER GENRES

This adventure is designed primarily for use with *Champions*. For heroic games, simply ignore the Demons and play up the street gang aspect of the adventure. In this case, the Demons really are just tough street punks, out to take control of the streets. For games set either in the era of pulp adventures or on fantasy worlds, the setting should be changed as appropriate, and the gangs may be replaced by small mobs, organized crime, or whatever else fits.

USING OTHER SUPPLEMENTS

Organizations Book 2: PRIMUS and DEMON is not required to play this module, but information from it can be easily incorporated into the adventure. Note that references to both DEMON and a group called the Circle are made in many of the Character Descriptions. If the GM does not have stats for these groups, or simply doesn't use them in his campaign, any villain group interested in magic may be substituted for DEMON. By the same logic, the Circle may be replaced by any magic-based hero group, or, if the GM has no such organization, the Champions may be used instead.

PLOT SUMMARY

The early sections of this adventure are a framework of encounters, all leading (through a series of increasingly bizarre events) to an ultimate climax on a mysterious island in Massachusetts.

Initially, something relatively minor, albeit disturbing, occurs in the GM's campaign city; someone seems to be uniting the various street gangs, and to be directing them intelligently and effectively. Ordinarily, the local police would be able to handle this, but none of the gang's victims are pressing charges, and few even want to talk about the situation!

Once the PCs become involved, they discover that the local gangs have been unified by a relatively new gang, a small one known as the "Demons." Up until this point, the greatest challenge facing the PCs is probably stopping the street thugs without seriously harming them (they are only normals, after all!). Now things change slightly; an encounter with this new "gang" reveals that their name was aptly chosen, for all six members are in fact, Demons!

Slowly, the PCs come to realize that these Demons bear striking resemblances to creatures from the horror stories of pulp novelist Howard Pickman; a race of beings he called the Forgotten gods. As the PCs become aware of this, they also discover that The Demons intend to open a gate to bring even more of their kind into our world!

Obviously, the PCs have to prevent this from happening. Ultimately, they confront the Demons on Serpent Head Island, to defeat the Demons once and for all.

HOW TO USE THIS BOOK

First, the GM should read through the entire adventure. To impart the proper mood during game play, the GM must have a thorough understanding of the scenario. Note that there are two distinct moods to this adventure; the first, dealing almost exclusively with street-level crime, should have a very gritty, realistic feel. This feel should shift slightly as the PCs move on to the second half of the adventure, as the role of the supernatural entities involved becomes more overt. This section should seem more surrealistic or fantastic in nature. The museum episode marks the dividing line between the two sections. (It is there that the Demons first reveal their full powers to the PCs.)

Second, the GM should examine the six major NPCs (the Demons), and familiarize himself with their capabilities, personalities, weaknesses, and strengths. The GM should feel free to change them for use in his campaign, if he feels it is needed. Also, if the PCs are significantly more powerful than the Demons, some supernatural villains may be added to their ranks to even things up; the best candidate would be Slug (from *Classic Enemies*), though Black Paladin, Dark Seraph (both also from *Classic Enemies*), and many of the Asesinos (from the *Champions* hardcover) would fit.

Finally, the GM will notice that several sections of this adventure are flexible, and may list a number of optional outcomes. Some of these options are determined solely by the actions of the PCs; a few, however, must be decided by the GM in advance. For example, during *the Final Battle*, a number of possible endings are listed in the text, but the PCs may (and should be encouraged to!) come up with their own ideas on handling this, perhaps ones requiring little or no NPC assistance.

VILLAIN MOTIVATION

Some GMs may find it unlikely for powerful creatures from another dimension, such as the Demons, to be employing mortal youths as agents. To fully understand the events of this Scenario, It is necessary to understand how the Demons think.

THE HISTORY OF THE DEMONS

At the dawn of time, the dimensional barriers were far more permeable than they are now. As man was first appearing on the Earth, many creatures freely roamed the seemingly infinite realms of existence.

One such creature was known as Tennigrath, one of the Nether gods. This horrible creature lives in an extra-dimensional realm far beyond the boundaries of reality. This creature is constantly spewing forth bits of matter which occasionally form into tangible objects or sentient creatures. One of Tennigrath's horrible creations was the creature known as Morgalis.

Morgalis served the Lord of The Void, but disliked remaining in his master's empty realm. So he travelled a lot, forging alliances with some races and making enemies of a number of others. During one of his sojourns, Morgalis discovered a world where an ape-like race was beginning to develop civilization. He returned and informed Tennigrath of this.

The Lord of the Void felt that perhaps on this young world he would be able to find beings that he could enslave. Morgalis obtained the assistance of a number of other creatures like himself, demons spewed forth from the realm of Chaos. Together, they staged an invasion of the world that would one day be called "Earth."

Morgalis was the first of these dimension travellers to contact the inhabitants of this world. He approached them as a great wizard, and many bowed down before his powers. With this "beachhead" established, the Lord of the Void and his fellow dimension travellers were able to subjugate a vast majority of the natives.

The Lord of the Void had no desire to remain on this world, however, so he charged his servant, the Wizard (as Morgalis had come to be called), with finding suitable slaves for him to take back. Realizing that the fragile creatures of this plane couldn't survive in the harsh environment of the Void, Morgalis began to cast protection spells upon them. Some of the more perceptive of the humans learned magic from watching the Wizard cast his wards.

This proved his undoing. The humans learned to use magic at a surprising rate, and in a short time, some of them were nearly the equals of their instructor. When they found out why the Wizard had cast the protective ward on them, they rebelled. The revolt was unexpected; thus the demons were caught unprepared. As a result, they were expelled from this dimension so forcefully that its boundaries became unpassable. Only creatures invited by a native of Earth could pass beyond this barrier. (For more information on ancient magicians and the origins of magic on Earth, see *Mystic Masters*.)

For many centuries, the Earth went by with no knowledge of these demons and their involvement in human development. Then, in the land that would one day be called America, a sacred ritual went wrong, accidentally allowing the Wizard to return to this world. The Wizard quickly slew the American Indian medicine man who had brought him here, and then summoned his master and their allies.

Unknown to the demons, the medicine man's spirit fled his body prior to its death to warn others of his error. In a nearby settlement, an old Shaman felt his cry, and quickly set about summoning those he would need to defeat these unwelcome visitors.

The demons had just arrived on Serpent Head Island, the site of the medicine man's error, when this Shaman and his hastily assembled army arrived. A fierce battle ensued. Finally, using three items of mystic power (An axe, a tuning fork and a cube), the Shaman expelled the Demons from this dimension and into one from which it was believed that they could never return.

A few centuries passed, during which time the Demons again faded from human memory. Then, while out hiking one day in the woods near Lake Perigannsett, a young New England man stumbled upon what appeared to be an ancient harvester's scythe in remarkably good condition. In Actuality, the scythe was actually a powerful weapon used by the Death Demon Alzol, but lost during the last of the demon wars. Pickman, however, believed it to be a simple antique or Indian artifact. Having an affinity for antiques, he took it home with him. That night, and every night for the rest of his life, this young man would have nightmares about that scythe and the creatures that had created it, for in truth it was the scythe that had been lost by the Death Demon. This man's name was Howard Pickman, and these dreams became the basis for his popular and chilling tales of the Forgotten Gods.

Most people (including Pickman himself) believed that these tales were mere fiction. Some, however, have suspected the truth — that something had given Pickman a glimpse of the Earth's long forgotten history.

Using one of his stories as a guide, members of DEMON discovered an ancient scroll that allowed them to bring one of these "Forgotten Gods" into our world. They also thought that they could control this creature.

They were wrong.

The Wizard returned, for the third time, to the Earth. This time he vowed that he would not be easily defeated. First he had to deal with the foolish "wizards" that summoned him, and then he would bring those of his brethren that he could contact to assist him. Most of the Forgotten Gods had been banished to a prison dimension beyond his ability to probe, so he was only able to summon a limited number of his brethren. Probing the minds of the few members of DEMON that he had permitted to live, he formulated a plan...

THE WIZARD'S PLAN

In the past the Demons had been defeated because they didn't properly understand humans. The Wizard surmised that he would need allies to help him learn the ways of this new era; allies that he could use, and then discard; allies that would provide a smoke-screen, covering his presence in this world until he was ready to strike.

DEMON did not seem like a good choice, as they obviously knew something of Demons and magic. Therefore he must look elsewhere for agents.

Normal human adults are likewise out of the question, since they tend to be difficult to control. The Wizard needed agents that were unrestrained by professional obligations and similar ties; agents that could "disappear" without causing a stir...

For these reasons, he has decided to look to the homeless and the young for sources of information, assistance, and possible hosts for his brethren. The street gangs of the city provided him with an ideal source of all three, and since they were already impressionable and rebellious, all he needed to do was tell them what they wanted to hear, and he could make them do anything.

With the aid of the street gangs, the Wizard can "feel out" this new era, and thus should be able to prevent a repeat of the disaster that befell his brethren centuries ago. By using a spell to alter his own features, the Wizard has become a leader to these youths, and this provides his "hunter-killer" Demon, Psycho, cover under which to seek out additional information sources.

OPTIONAL SUMMONING

As an option, The Wizard needs to use mortals as hosts to summon his brethren into this dimension. If this option is used, all of the other Demons are initially inhabiting bodies of street kids. If any Demon other than the Wizard is slain, that Demon is met later in the body of another gang member!

At first, this system of body stealing (called soul riding by the Demons) might seem ideal. However, most human bodies are far too frail to contain the powerful and evil spirits of Demons. Any body being possessed by a demon should begin to deteriorate within a week of the possession. Essentially, the Demon's spirit is destroying the body which contains it.

In game terms, any normal human possessed by a demon will lose 1 BODY and 2 COM for each week that he is possessed. Once the victim's BODY total reaches 0, he dies and the Demon must find a new victim to possess.

DANGER ON THE STREETS

A number of short encounters, each designed for a small group of Player Characters, are provided here. Each of these encounters should indicate to the PCs that a disturbing trend is afoot — one that merits investigation. All of these encounters are optional, though it is advised that a few be used. Some encounters may be combined, and most do not have to occur in any particular order.

If the GM finds that it is difficult to run these encounters with small groups of players, he can write up some of the street kids, and give them to players who have no heroes involved in the current episode. This not only prevents these players from being bored, but also eases some of the roleplaying and book-keeping chores, and may even provide the players running heroes with a more challenging encounter! (GMs should be careful, however, not to force the players to run NPCs when they really want to be running their own characters.)

During these mini-adventures, the Wizard is "feeling" out his new world, while increasing the strength of his hold on the gangs and generally making a nuisance of himself.

ENCOUNTER 1: DNPC IN PERIL

Remember the scene in the Superman movie where Clark and Lois are cornered by a band of robbers in a back alley in Metropolis?

A PC in his civilian ID and one (or more) of his DNPCs are wandering along one fine day when a group of street punks (some wearing jackets reading "Sharks," others in jackets reading "Hawks") approach them, asking for a handout. Once the kids corner their marks, one of the Hawks pulls out a pistol and menaces the PC while the others gang members begin to search the PC's companions. The following is a brief description of the thugs involved:

- A Hawk with a .45 Automatic (1d6 +1 RKA, +1 OCV, +1 STUN Multiple, 7 charges)
- Two Sharks armed with Chains (3d6 HA with 1" Stretching)
- One Hawk with 15 STR and a wooden board (+2d6 HA, 1 ½ handed), who acts as leader.
- A number of street-fighters, all Hawks, with the Dirty Infighting Martial Arts style. One per DNPC involved.

This encounter can occur in any back alley or deserted area of the city, and may be repeated. The challenge here is for the hero to protect the DNPC and to survive without revealing his Secret Identity (Of course, street thugs will not challenge heroes with Public IDs, unless they outnumber such heroes by a margin of at least 4 to 1!).

ENCOUNTER 2: THE OLD LADY

A PC is passing a back alley somewhere in the city and observes a group of five toughs wearing red and orange clothing (they are Predators.) The thugs are menacing an old lady. However, she is a skilled combatant and can generally take care of herself. If the heroes do not interfere, she will take out four of the five thugs before she is finally taken down.

If the PCs do not attempt to save the old woman, they are not being very heroic. Have the whole encounter witnessed by an unfriendly reporter who will write a scathing article against the heroes (complete with pictures).

The hero may have a hard time living this one down!

If the hero helps the old lady, he discovers that she is Agatha Baxter, better known as "Granny Judo." She runs a local home for wayward children, and she had approached these thugs in order to see if they knew where one of her missing boys, Rico Sarducci, was. Rico is constantly getting himself into trouble with his old friends (the street gang known as the Studs). Whenever he goes out with his old friends, she usually finds him at the police station, a few days later.

The only problem is that he left with his friends over a week ago, and still hasn't turned up. Granny Judo is worried. If the PC offers to help her search for him, it will be some time before any leads turn up...

***Note:** These thugs really have no desire to mug the old lady; she is in their territory asking silly questions; to them, roughing her up is merely a matter of pride. A quick-thinking hero (or one with a high Presence) could bring this encounter to a peaceful conclusion, and may gain both information on the Demons and the eternal respect of Granny Judo while doing so!*

ENCOUNTER 3: ANGELS IN HEAVEN

Baren's Jewelry is the setting for this encounter. A group of five girls all wearing blue denim skirts and white jackets emblazoned with the single word "Angels" enter the store in the early afternoon. The only other person present is Adam Baren, the stores owner (a normal man with 11 DEX, PS: Jeweler 11- and Trading 14-).

After looking around for a while, one of the girls (identified by the others as Vanessa) draws a gun (.38; 1d6+1 RKA) and demands that Baren put all of the jewelry in the store in the shopping bags that the other girls have brought along.

The Angels are not the most serious of street gangs and are really not into theft. Should any heroes with high COM (21+) scores attempt to talk to the girls, they could earn the Angels respect (if the hero is female) or adoration (if the hero is male.) Such PCs could bring this encounter to a peaceful conclusion.

If the PCs simply attack the Angels, the girls will attempt to flee. They dislike combat and are deathly afraid of going to jail. If cornered, the girls will put up a brief fight, but will eventually surrender when it is clear they are outclassed.

If a character emerges from this encounter on speaking terms with any (or all) of the girls, that character discovers that the girls were put up to this robbery by Vanessa's new boyfriend, the leader of a new local gang called the Demons."He's not much to look at, but he does know how to treat a girl."

BAREN'S JEWELRY

Baren is motivated solely by greed, and often attempts to palm off cheap or costume jewelry on unsuspecting customers. Should violence occur, he attempts to help heroes save his store (there is a .45 Automatic (1d6+1 RKA) in the cash register.)

Vanessa is greedy and obnoxious. The other girls simply idolize her. Vanessa will be as abrasive to the heroes as she thinks she can get away with. She is attempting to impress the Demons as well as her girls.

Use the stats for the "typical" gang leader, but Vanessa has a .38 Special (1d6 +1 RKA, 6 charges) and two levels with it instead of Dirty Infighting.

If the PCs arrest the Angels, Morgalis visits Baren and threatens him. He will refuse to press charges against the girls and will not testify. As he was the only witness to the crime, and the owner of the store, it will be impossible to hold the Angels without his testimony. If the PCs ask why he refuses to testify, he claims that it's obvious that the girls have learned their lesson and he's sure they won't try it again.

Only under Telepathy is the truth discovered. He was approached by a young man who talked to him, during which time Adam found himself becoming more fearful, until finally he agreed to anything the youth said.

Barren testifies only under hypnosis or Mind Control (neither of which is permissible in most courts). Note that all wronged parties, except PCs and some mugging victims, suffer similar fates throughout these early episodes. The Wizard needs his agents, and does everything he can to protect them while they permit him to gain the information he needs.

ENCOUNTER 4: BAD MEDICINE

It is an ordinary afternoon at Drew's Drugs. Up to 2d6 Customers are present (possibly one or more being heroes in Civilian IDs, perhaps with a few DNPCs), and everything is going quite well. Kevin Drew is manning the cash register, while his father, Brian Drew, is filling prescriptions in the back. Suddenly, a group of teenagers wander in. One pulls a gun on Kevin, demanding all of the cash in his register, while the others wander about the store demanding the same of the customers and taking anything that catches their fancy.

Obviously, this has to stop!

DREW'S DRUGS

Kevin Drew is a very business-minded and courageous young man. He does not know that his father refuses to keep their pistol loaded, and will attempt to get this if he sees a reasonable opportunity. His father immediately "knuckles under" during a robbery to prevent people from getting hurt. Brian is also a very observant person, however, and constantly takes mental notes on anyone causing trouble in his shop.

The "assault force" consists of the following kids:

One youth armed with a .41 Magnum (1 ½d6 RKA, +1 STUN Multiple, -1 OCV, 6 charges), two Chain Fighters (+3d6 HA w/1" Stretching), and up to six (2 per PC, maximum of 6) kids who know Dirty Infighting.

The Chain fighters are from a gang known as the "Sharks," all of whom wear (stolen) soft leather clothes, and the Street Fighters (those with Dirty Infighting) are members of a gang reputed to be bloody rivals of theirs, the "Rockers." Rockers dress outlandishly, have multicolored hair, and wear tastelessly applied make-up. The gunman is Rico Sarducci, a member of a gang from the "other side" of the city called the "Studs" (mentioned in Encounter #2, above).

If captured, these kids state that this robbery was inspired by a speech made by the leader of a new gang in the city. This gang leader, who calls himself "The Wizard," says that the gangs possess enough power to take anything that they want or need, and — if they set aside their petty differences and work together — that they can reshape the world into a paradise where all will have plenty, and adults will be unable force their desires on teens!

ENCOUNTER 5: DEXTER UPTON MEMORIAL HIGH, AFTER HOURS

Late at night, a group of teens, all members of The Back Street Brawlers, attempt to break into their high school and mess the place up. This force consists of three gang members armed with black-jacks, each possessing a number of Skills helpful in staging a break-in (Lockpicking, Security Systems, Stealth, etc.), plus the leader of the gang ("Stick," see the gang write-up), plus one additional kid with Dirty Infighting for each PC hero.

The youths climb the fence around the back of the building, disarm the alarm system, pick the locks on the front doors and break into the school. They will then try and do as much damage to the place as possible, pausing briefly to steal anything they see that could be valuable.

PCs can become involved if any of the alarms go off, or simply by seeing either the gang members in the school yard or perhaps by spotting the open door or mysterious lights inside the building. The gang members have been emboldened by the words of the leader of a new gang in the area, who has informed them that "schools are places where the adults mess with kids' heads and force them to believe what the adults want them to."

This gang leader, known only as the Wizard, asked them to vandalize the place as a symbol of their values. Unknown to the teens, this break-in was actually engineered by the Wizard to provide a smoke-screen to cover his own break-in at a local library. Once the Back Street Brawlers have had fifteen minutes at the school, he gives the police an anonymous "tip" about them, and then proceeds to Encounter #6.

DEXTER UPTON MEMORIAL HIGH SCHOOL

NPCS

Old Irving Smith is the school's night security guard. He has been employed by them for 35 years, and is near retirement age. He is poorly equipped (a Normal with Age 60+, 11 DEX, a nightstick (+2d6 HA), and FAM: Firearms). Irving dislikes violence, preferring to either talk intruders out of acting, or to ignore them. He is probably either in a classroom (sleeping), or off somewhere talking to one of the night janitors (all of whom are normals with as little or as much personality as the GM sees fit to give them).

INSIDE THE SCHOOL

All outside walls are concrete, while immobile interior walls are composed of cinder blocks. Mobile walls (denoted by broken lines) are DEF 3 BODY 2 (Pasteboard). Due to space limitations, full descriptions of school rooms could not be provided. However, the following locations are suggested as being interesting place where a fight could occur: Machine Shop, Cafeteria, Locker Rooms, School Gym and the School Theater.

This is the only encounter in this section where the Wizard actually permits his "followers" to be arrested.

ENCOUNTER 6: THE LIBRARY AFFAIR

Three gang members (two Hawks, and one Stud, all with the skills Lockpicking and Security Systems, plus two with Computer Programming) have been asked to help the Wizard break into a local library. He claims that libraries are "just another place where the youth is being brainwashed." He has informed the gangs that he intends to break into one and trash it.

However, his actual goal is to find a pair of books that Psycho spotted here the night before. One relates a number of legends of Pre-European New England and goes into detail about the imprisonment of a group of "Evil Spirits" by a band of American Indian medicine men. The other contains a number of more contemporary stories from that same region. The story that interests the Wizard the most is one about an author who stumbled on an ancient scythe while hiking in the woods near Lake Perigannsett, Massachusetts.

The Wizard is interested in both of these books, for he feels (correctly) that they contain clues to finding the information he needs to free the Lord of the Void and his brethren. Thus, he plans to steal these books.

There are many ways in which PCs can become involved here; PCs may observe the break-in attempt, find out about it from contacts in the streets, or feel that something is wrong (Danger Sense) at the library and investigate. Of course, PCs involved at Dexter Upton Memorial High (see above) cannot participate here.

Known only to the Wizard, Psycho is already in the library, and he escapes with the second of the books once the door is opened. It takes the Wizard a few minutes to locate the other book. If PCs interrupt the robbery, he attempts to get out of sight of everyone, grab the book, and teleport away. The gang members attempt to do as much damage as possible and get out quickly. They try to avoid combat.

If any of the kids are captured, they mention that they saw a large cat run out of the building when the doors were opened. One of the kids believes that the cat had a book in its mouth.

Investigation reveals that a book on the legends of precolonial New England is missing, as is a text on New England Folklore. Of course, chances are that a great number of books were destroyed in the break in, so this loss may go completely unnoticed. It takes the library about a week to locate additional copies of any lost books.

At the GM's option, Psycho could have torn the cover page of his book, and thus left some or all of it behind.

ENCOUNTER 7: TEACHER, TEACHER

If one of the PCs or a DNPC is a school teacher, they notice that there has been an increase in absences among teen aged students. Initially, this increase is among the less reputable of the students, and is thus overlooked.

Soon, however, some of the better students are also missing class far more frequently than usual, and when these students do show up, they tend to be more rebellious than is normal.

Any direct questions meet with either blank stares, threats, or actual violence. One teacher (an NPC associated with one of the heroes) was brutally beaten by some students for moving the due date of a term paper up a few days!

This teacher believes that there was a student in the room that he had never seen before, and that this student actually started the violence. Unfortunately, the teacher suffers from occasional memory lapses due to a concussion he suffered during the incident, and may not recall the event correctly. (Actually, Enforcer accompanied one of the leaders of a local gang to school that day, and incited the riot himself, even landing one of the first punches on the teacher!)

ENCOUNTER 8: REVERSAL!

If one of the earlier robbery episodes has occurred and PCs have interfered with two or more (apparently) unrelated plots of the Demons, one of the individuals who initially refused to testify suddenly decides to press charges against the heroes! The store owner explains that he was accosted by one of the PCs (preferably one with a violent or vigilante reputation); the hero demanded protection money from him. The street kids attempted to stop the hero, but were outmatched. When the hero heard the police sirens, he claimed that he caught the kids robbing the store. The store owner will say that another hero has threatened him with violence if this information was ever revealed, but he can no longer stand to see such an injustice remain unpunished.

To make this situation worse, the vendor actually believes that the situation he just described actually took place, and will be unable to rest until justice has been served. The poor shopkeeper has had his memory altered (as have any other available eyewitnesses to the initial robbery), courtesy of the Wizard.

The leader of the Demons is angry with the heroes for interfering with his plans, and wants them out of the way. The PCs are now faced with a dilemma: they can either accept punishment for crimes they did not commit, submit to a long trial which may end with their incarceration, or become fugitives from the law until the Demons have been finally dealt with.

This encounter is meant to give the PCs an indication of the power that they are up against, and should add a good deal of tension to the campaign.

ENCOUNTER 9: ANYTHING ELSE

GMs should feel free to set up situations similar to the ones described above. Other possibilities for interesting encounters include:

A. PCs hear about an impending gang war and arrive to stop it. They find either nothing, two supposedly hostile gangs "partying" together, or perhaps a rally held by the Demons.

B. Assuming that DEMON is being used in the GMs campaign, once the PCs are aware of the existence of gang called the Demons, they may assume that a link between them and the criminal organization DEMON exists. Scouring the City, they stumble upon the Demonlair where The Wizard was initially summoned. What they find there is a devastated Demonlair filled with corpses. This structure could possibly serve as a temporary base for the Demons, and a few of them may be in residence, if the GM so desires.

If the GM wishes, one of the DEMON guards who was present when the Wizard was summoned might have escaped the massacre. He would be badly wounded and hiding somewhere in the city. If the PCs can find him, he could provide them with some kind of information concerning the Demons.

C. Deciding that his youth army needs better weapons, The Wizard may stage an assault on a local weapon shop or police station. This could easily escalate into a complex hostage situation, should PCs become involved, and may end with well-armed opposition for the PCs.

D. The PCs may attempt to infiltrate the gangs to obtain information on the Demons. PCs who are (or can look like) teens should have little trouble, but note that these heroes may find themselves swept along with the gangs. Also, there is a chance that the PC "mole" will be discovered, and Mind Controlled (or worse!) by the Wizard.

ENCOUNTER 10: CONFRONTATION

The main function of this encounter is to reveal the true nature(s) of the Demons to the PCs suddenly and (hopefully) without warning.

Eventually, the PCs realize that a small gang called the Demons, led by a man known as the Wizard is loose in their City. They've been uniting street gangs, collecting wealth and possessions from people around the city, and corrupting the city's youth.

Once the PCs are aware of this, either they will seek out the Demons for a "little discussion," or, a small group of heroes — or a lone hero — is approached by the Wizard, Runt, and Enforcer at some point, in a back alley.

The Wizard greets the PCs: "So, you are the thorn that has been trying to wedge itself into our sides! I would suggest that you stick to pounding on supervillains; you can handle them. We are way out of your league, my pathetic friend." (Throughout the Wizard's speech, Runt parrots most of what the Wizard says, adding in a "yes" or similar statement and an occasional giggle.)

Once he finishes his speech, the Wizard turns to the large youth at his side and says "Enforcer, show them the error of their ways." If there are several heroes present, or the hero is very tough, Runt is also be ordered into action.

Enforcer approaches the PCs and attempts to rough them up. He (probably) fails, and is rendered unconscious. Soon, however, given his recovery, he revives, reverts to his true form and again assaults the heroes, laughing the whole time.

Runt, if he is involved, behaves in a similar manner. If needed, other Demons may be included. The PCs may win this fight, but it should be a hard-earned victory, and the Wizard should escape (via Teleport.)

The Demons fight until either they are beaten, the PCs run, or all of the PCs are unconscious. If the PCs attempt to flee, the Wizard lets them, assuming that they are too frightened to oppose him later. If the PCs are defeated, the Wizard will hang them from a nearby wall and use their own blood to leave a message for them:

"DEMONS RULE THE STREETS"

Should reinforcements arrive, the Demons flee; they wish to have as few people as possible know their true natures. The Wizard tells them: "When you see him, be sure to thank Pickman for me," before the Demons walk of, laughing.

ENCOUNTER 11: RICO'S STORY

Note: *This encounter may make no sense to the PCs if they have not met Rico in the Bad Medicine (Encounter #4) episode, above. Note also that Encounter #2 (The Old Lady) ties into this one.*

Sometime after Encounter #10, a nervous Rico Sarducci comes running up to one or more heroes. He is breathless, terrified, and begs the PCs for protection. If the heroes promise to help him, he begins to talk.

This is his story:

Recently one of Rico's friends was arrested (during the break in at the school, to be exact). Rico had planned on asking the Wizard to get his friend out of prison, and went to the old building that the Demons use when they wish to address the street gangs.

Arriving there, he overheard the Wizard and Psycho discussing something. From what he heard, they were planning to remove something from a local museum. Rico did not stick around long, though: as he listened (waiting for a chance to address the Wizard alone), he saw something that terrified him. Psycho was not a man, but a creature... more horrible then anything Rico could have possibly imagined.

As he talks with the PCs, Rico remembers having read about a creature that matched the description of what he saw at the old building.

The description came from a story he encountered a few years ago. It was a horror story by Howard Pickman, entitled "Hunter's Moon."

This information should allow the PCs to anticipate the Demons' next major move...

RESEARCH

Once the PCs are at least partially aware of the nature of their opposition, they should wonder what the Demons motivations are.

The following list contains a number of subjects which the PCs may wish to look into. These are listed in the following format: Subject: Possible Source (Appropriate Skills), and Information that can be discovered.

Characters without appropriate Skills (even if using Computer Programming) have a base 8- roll to research a given topic successfully. Note also that PCs with appropriate Contacts or Favors could convince other people to do research for them.

DEMONS, MYTHICAL (GENERAL):

Most large libraries, several private libraries, or personal libraries. (KS: Demonology, KS: or SC: Occult Sciences, PS: Student, PS: Library Use).

1. Most Demons are vulnerable to Magical attacks. Many are vulnerable to silver or iron weapons, as well.
2. Throughout the ages, a number of Demon-worshipping cults have existed. Currently, only a few are known, foremost among these are DEMON and any other occult organizations in the GMs campaign.
3. A number of Demons have been described in popular literature. Many of these Demons closely match Christian archetypes with bestial features, horns, hooves and bat wings. Some books, however, discuss Demons of a very different kind. These creature tend to be more horrible and typically resemble blobs with wings and tentacles. Some of the most striking examples of this can be found in the stories of the Forgotten Gods. The principal author of these stories was pulp novelist Howard Pickman.
4. Many occult texts have references to a race of giant, skeletal monsters, armed with magical weapons. These legends also say that a number of these weapons have fallen into the hands of mortals, and have brought both great power and disaster to their wielders. These creatures were considered a type of demon.

DEMONS, MYTHICAL (SPECIFIC):

Sources and Skills as above.

"Grim Reaper" (also available to PCs following up on Clue 4, above)**:** Occult researchers theorize the existence of a race of giant, skeletal, weapon-wielding monsters. A few such researchers have attempted to catalog these creatures, and among those catalogued is a scythe wielding Demon named Alzol.

"Elementals": Numerous texts make references to elementals, or living embodiments of fire, water, earth and air. Most of these creatures were believed to be unbiased in nature, but some were tainted with the touch of elder gods. These creatures became demonic in nature and used their control of the elements to plague humanity.

"Deceivers": A great deal of old folk tales involving Demons portray the creatures as unholy salesmen, willing to give their victims what ever they desire in return for their immortal souls.

Obviously, some of this information is not appropriate to the adventure. GMs should feel free to include other red herrings.

HOWARD PICKMAN:

The best source on Pickman himself is the museum named after him, although most libraries will have some information on him (KS: Literature, KS: Occult, PS: Student, PS: Library Research).

1. Pickman was a writer and illustrator for a number of "Weird" (Horror) Tales, during the twenties and early thirties. He died in 1937.
2. Pickman was born in 1893, to a woman who's family had a history of Insanity. Dr. Sebastian Poe once claimed that this family demonstrated evidence of latent psychic mutations.
3. In an interview that the author gave just before he died, Pickman described how in the early 1900's, he discovered an odd scythe that appeared immune to the effects of time. While he possessed it, he had terrible nightmares. Many of these nightmares eventually became the basis for his tales of the malevolent Forgotten Gods, creatures who once ruled this world, but were banished from it, and now seek to return and destroy mankind.
4. The scythe that Pickman found, along with a complete collection of his works, can be found at a local museum named in his honor.
5. A number of occultists have theorized that the scythe that Pickman found once belonged to a Demon (given the nightmares that possession of it brought on), and that his "Forgotten Gods" really did exist at one time, long ago in Earth's past.

THE FORGOTTEN GODS:

The best sources on these beings is Pickman's own novels, though Dunham University (see below) has a great deal of information on them, as do many other libraries, especially those oriented towards the occult (PS: Library Research, PS: Student, KS; Occult Literature, KS or SC: Occult).

1. Many of the Demons bear striking resemblances to some of the Forgotten Gods from Pickman's "fiction."
2. In one of his stories, Pickman detailed a ritual to summon the Forgotten Gods to this world. This story, entitled "Scavenger Hunt," involves a hero, Roger Carson (an apparent alter-ego for the author who appears in a number of his stories), who races against members of an evil cult, seeking a set of three artifacts. Carson fails to prevent the cultists from finding these items (an axe, a leather sack, and a red crystal cube.) and finally confronts the cultists at the sight of an ancient shrine. He interrupts their spell, but is destroyed in the process. The final passage of the story goes as follows:

"Fearing the consequences of the spell, Roger tackled the High Priest of the cult, and wrestled him to the ground. Taking the axe from atop the altar stone, Roger hefted it over his head.

A look of utter terror showed upon the face of the dark priest. At first, Roger thought that the priest feared for his own existence. Then the priest spoke.

"You may have spared the world, at least for now, but you have doomed us all!"

The priest pointed upwards, and Roger turned to follow the gesture. The dark funnel was closing, but something was there...Something that reached out for the men on the island with what might have been an arm.

The arm swept the island clean, and all present were drawn into the formless void as the funnel closed forever."

The story indicates that the axe was found in the Arctic Circle, the cube in Japan, and the pouch somewhere near New York City. Should the PCs research these items (through local libraries, especially noting news reports), they discover that items matching the descriptions of the pouch and the cube have been discovered in the locations that the story mentioned, although the cube was recently stolen by VIPER. The pouch is on display in a museum in New York (or some other major city of the GMs choosing).

AMERICAN INDIAN LEGENDS (MASSACHUSETTS):

Most Libraries (KS: History, KS: American History, KS: American Mythology/Folklore, KS: American Indians, PS: Library Research, PS: Student).

Researching this will turn up a number of legends. PCs who are aware of Pickman's connection with the Demons will be able to single out those dealing with the Lake Perigannsett region. There are two legends about this region; the first explains the name of the Island of the Serpent Father, and the second deals with a number of ghosts that appeared there long before the advent of white man upon American shores.

The first legend provides little real useful information, but PCs who read through the second will notice some interesting facts. First of all, many of the "ghosts" which the legend describes closely resemble the Demons the PCs have clashed with. Secondly, the text describes the Demons being driven back into the spirit plane by a powerful shaman using three items of power: a stone axe, a stone, "Y" shaped fork and strange glowing cube.

LAKE PERIGANNSETT OR SERPENT HEAD ISLAND:

Most libraries (KS or SC: Geography, AK: Massachusettses or Northeastern U.S., PS: Library Use, PS: Student).

In addition to notes on climate, native life, etc., researching this will turn up the following:

1. The American Indian Myths described above, and
2. The fact that most of Pickman's stories are set either in this region or in the nearby city of Dunham.

STOLEN ITEMS:

Newspaper offices (PS: Library Use, PS: Journalism, Conversation), Police (Conversation, Contact Police), and the site of the theft (Conversation, Criminology).

Such research will turn up a list of stolen items, the apparent identity of the thieves, and a list of possible motives. This varies according from encounter to encounter, and each list must be formulated by the GM as needed. The following is a sample list, and what it might imply:

If the PCs obtain a list of the books that were taken from the library (episode #6), and look for connecting points, they should discover that the Demons have an interest in early American history, especially that of the New England area.

Using the above as guidelines, the results of other research can be fabricated as needed.

HUNTING FOR MAGIC

ONE FINE DAY AT THE MUSEUM

The raid on the library (Encounter #6) provides the Wizard with a surplus of information. The first piece of data that he discovers is the location of Enforcer's scythe, as well as the location of a complete collection of Pickman's works, which should contain the spell he needs. Both items are currently in the possession of the Howard Pickman Museum of Natural History, a small museum in or near the campaign city. The Wizard has Psycho scout out the museum, to determine how well it is guarded. With this information, he plans to assault the museum. He feels that the raid should go unopposed.

If the PCs are exceptionally alert and willing to perform a bit of research, they should be able to anticipate (perhaps with the aid of Deduction) the intentions of the Demons. In this case, they may suspect that both the scythe and complete set of the author's writings (on display at the Howard Pickman museum) are of some importance to the Demons. Realizing this, the PCs may plan an ambush for the Demons, or they may attempt to obtain these items for themselves.

If they choose the latter option, they find that legal measures prove fruitless, as Harvey Randell, the current curator, does not permit any materials to leave the museum. The PCs are free to examine both the Scythe and the stories during the museum's hours of operation, however. If the PCs decide to use illegal methods to obtain these items, they just happen to do so on the same night that the Demons do...

If the heroes do not anticipate the plans of the Demons, they can become involved in this episode in any number of ways. A hero with Danger Sense might feel Psycho's presence nearby. This should prompt an investigation. Also, the assault force may be unable to defeat all of the alarms, or they may be spotted by alert heroes on patrol before (or as) they reach the museum. A character with Unluck (or both Luck and Unluck) who flies past the museum may find a sudden air current slamming him through a skylight right into the lap of either a security guard or the assault force. Characters with Streetwise or street-level Contacts may also discover that someone is planning to break into the Howard Pickman Museum and steal some rare books.

The Demon's goal in this Scenario is to obtain the scythe and some of Pickman's rarer works. The outcome of this scenario could be very important to future encounters, so the GM should be careful while running it. Should Enforcer recover his scythe, then he will be significantly more powerful. If the PCs and the Demons are already well matched, this encounter could throw that balance off. If the PCs are much tougher than the Demons, then the GM should probably let Enforcer recover the scythe just to even things up. If the heroes are already weaker than their opponents, then the GM should go to great lengths to make sure the Demons do not recover the scythe.

Of course, the scythe is not the only item here that interests the Demons; they also seek the collection of Pickman's works in the library. If the Wizard fails to obtain them here, he will be able to locate copies in other museums specializing in occult works, but he'd rather kill two (or more) birds with one stone. Details of the museum can be found below.

HOWARD PICKMAN MUSEUM

HISTORY

After a particularly vivid nightmare, Howard Pickman found himself questioning the origin of mankind.

To assuage his own doubts, Pickman contacted a friend of his, a professor of Natural History (one Franklin Jacob Steurt) who had recently moved to the City, and offered to pay him to investigate mankind's beginnings.

Pickman died shortly after, and never knew that his money financed a small but successful museum. In his will, he left a complete set of his writings and the Scythe that he had discovered several years earlier to Steurt, and these have become permanent exhibits.

NPCS

In a night-time scenario, the museum is populated by relatively faceless security guards (they patrol, drink coffee, discuss family problems and how boring their jobs are, and do little else on a normal evening). During a break-in, however, these guards are highly efficient (at least against normal criminals). The guards are Skilled Normals with small handguns (1d6 RKAs) and night sticks (+3d6 HA.)

During the day, the museum is frequented by many visiting scholars and families of tourists

KEY

All Exterior walls are concrete, and interior walls in all but the most recent section (the Library Wing) are sturdy oak (DEF 4 BODY 3). The walls in the new wing are of slightly cheaper wood.

1. Statues: At each of these locations is a stone statue of lions (DEF 7 BODY 5}.

2. Entrance: This area is tastefully decorated with 18th century furniture and medieval wall hangings. The area listed as 2a is a coat-check room.

3. Information Desk: Two padded plastic chairs and a wood and steel rack of pamphlets are here. The pamphlets cover current and touring exhibits, as well as area amusement parks, golf courses, and a health club on the shore of Lake Perigannsett in Massachusetts.

4. Public Restrooms: 4a. is a women's rest-room, and 4b. is a men's rest-room.

5. Drinking Fountain: A Giant Clam Shell (DEF 4 BODY 3) and Drinking Fountain.

6. Gift Shop: Several "tourist" items are on display here, along with replicas of some exhibits.

7. Taxidermy Display: Each case contains stuffed animals. Most notable among these are a horse, a bear, a crocodile, and a large python.

8. Repair and Construction Shop: A disassembled duck-billed dinosaur covers the mobile table (8b.). The west wall holds several steel filing cabinets, and parts of several incomplete exhibits clutter the floor.

9. Prehistoric Animal Displays: These displays hold a number of small skeletons and plaques describing them, their habitats, and any unusual features.

10. Epoch Diorama: This room contains a number of plastic dioramas depicting the various epoches of time.

11. Skeleton of a Brontosaurus: (DEF 4, BODY 24).

12. Triceratops Skeleton: (DEF 4 BODY 18). The horns are effectively a +5d6 HA.

13. Two Small Dinosaurs: One egg-eater (DEF 4 BODY 12) and one "sail-backed" (DEF 4 BODY 10).

14. Tyrannosaurus Skeleton: (DEF 4 BODY 20).

15. Farmer's wagon: It is heavy, wooden, and, due to its age, extremely fragile.

16. Indian Costumes: These cases hold a number of old costumes and masks from various cultures which Pickman refers to in his books. Most prominent are the Perigannsett Indian items.

17. Writing Tools: A number of ancient writing tools and samples of ancient texts are here. These are possibly the most valuable items here, and are held in a solid steel case with Questonite facing.

18. Plate Barding (horse armor)

19. Armory: A plexiglass case (DEF 4 BODY 2) holds several examples of mediaeval weaponry. These items are more for show then anything else. However, should a character wish to use them as weapons, most will serve as 1d6+1 HKAs.

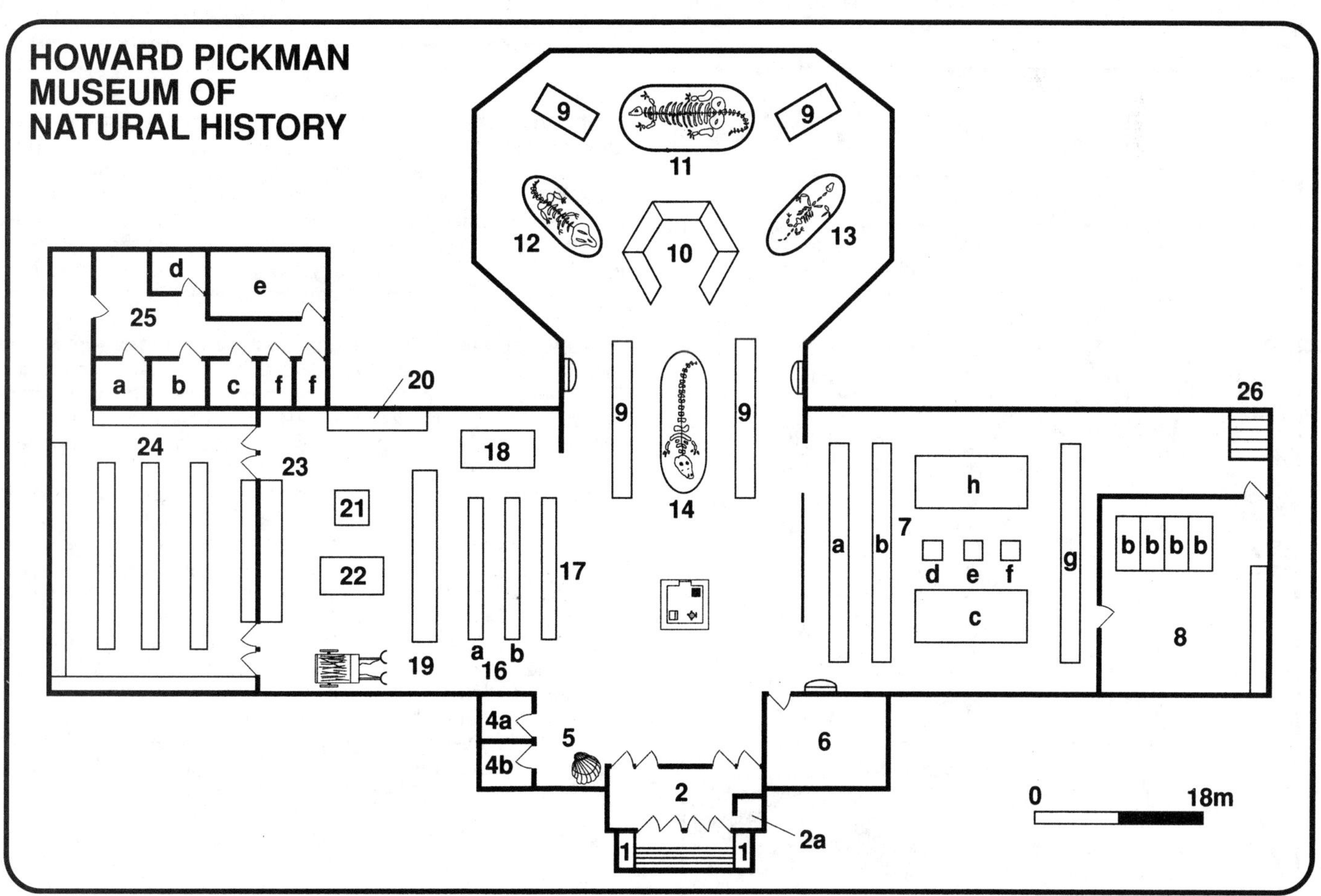

20. Body Armor: This case contains several examples of human armor, ranging from simple skins to a bullet-proof vest employed during the twenties. The case is simple glass. (The armor is real and ranges from DEF 1 all the way up to DEF 8. Armored suits take a full turn to put on.)

21. Roman Gladiator: A mannikin dressed as a Roman gladiator is displayed here. It holds a Pilum (Roman lead-shafted spear; 1 ½d6 RKA + a 2d6, Entangle with no Defense), a Gladius (1 ½d6 HKA). The mannikin has DEF 4, but it also has a Roman shield, that adds 4 DEF on an 11- roll. A total of 6 BODY destroys it. (Note that this is one of the many interesting Automatons that the Wizard's spells can create here.)

22. Agricultural Tools: A collection of colonial agricultural items are on display in this case.

23.Agricultural Weaponry: This case shows a number of agricultural tools and their weapon derivations. Items on display include such odd items as an Okinawan rice-flail and the nunchaku developed from it. The prominent item here is one of the items which the Demons seek, the Scythe of Alzol. A plaque beneath this display indicates that it was donated by the late Howard Pickman, who discovered it while out hiking one day near Lake Perigannsett.

24. Library: Hardwood shelves hold numerous texts on history, archaeology, and anthropology. These shelves also contain the only complete collection of Pickman's writings (including letters written to his friends). Most of the volumes here are both valuable and fragile.

25. Offices: Room 25 itself is a small waiting room, while 25a. contains those museum records not stored in area #8, above. 25b. is a small office for the curator's secretary. 25c is break room for the security guards, and 25d contains a number of monitors set up to scan the museum. These monitors are fairly sloppily manned, so there is only a 12- chance (modified by Stealth rolls, of course) that any break-in is noticed. 25e. is the curator's office, and both rooms marked 25f. are single-person rest rooms.

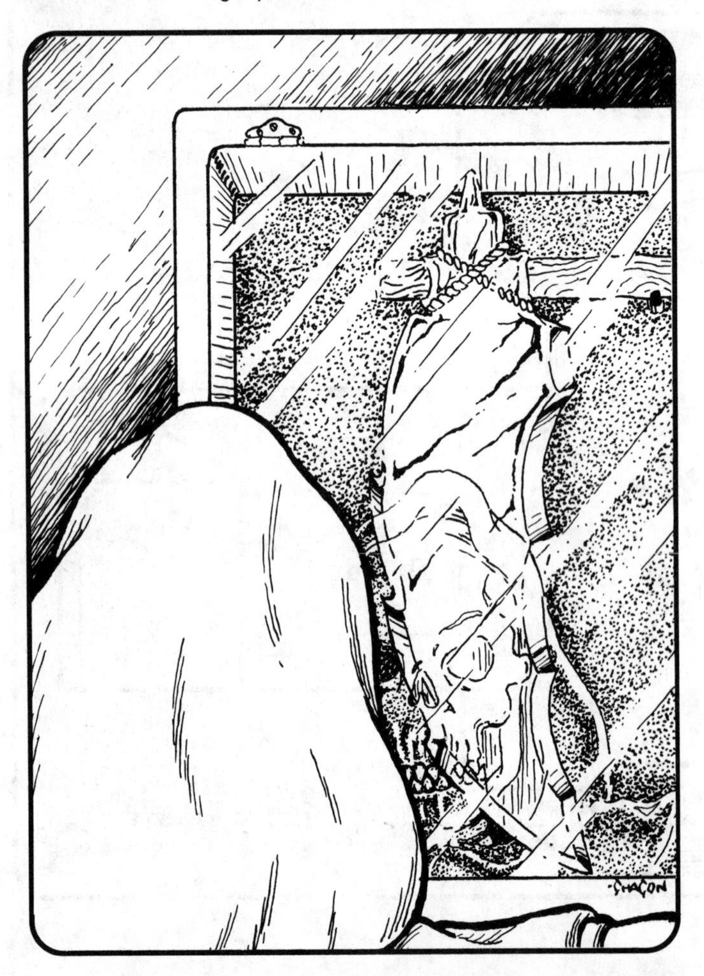

COMBAT IN THE MUSEUM

Should a fight break out here, security forces become involved after the first Turn of combat. They are not really prepared to deal with the threat of superpowered intruders, so their first move will be to call in reinforcements from the local police station. Unfortunately, these reinforcements won't arrive for 7 Turns. The security forces will attempt to hide behind cover and use their pistols to hold off the intruders until the police can arrive. Unless the PCs have received specific permission to be in the museum, they too are considered intruders.

During the battle, the Demons break up their forces into three "groups." The first group, consisting of Psycho, Blade, Torch, and Runt engages the heroes. Psycho and Torch also attempt to attract the attention of security forces. The Demons believe that the guards will cause problems for the heroes who feel obligated to protect them from harm. Enforcer breaks off on his own to retrieve his scythe, and rejoins the other four after doing so. The Wizard heads off to the library along with all of the street kids he has brought along (about two per PC), to obtain the set of Pickman's writings.

Once he has the books, he uses an area affect teleport (created with his pool; 20" Teleport, affects one hex, inflicts 6d6 Normal on all using it if a 15- Activation Roll is failed), to escape, and then contacts Runt through their Mindlink (which Runt keeps active during the battle) to inform him of their success. At this point, the Demons all attempt to flee and regroup.

During the fight, Runt boasts that the heroes, even if they do survive this battle, don't have a prayer of stopping the Wizard's brilliant plan; once the Forgotten Gods return to this world, the PCs will be sorry that they ever opposed the Demons!

SCAVENGER HUNT

Now that The Enforcer either has his scythe, or has lost it "forever" (a relative term in the world of comics; he may later attempt to retrieve it, especially if the PCs leave it unguarded), and the Demons also possess the information they require, they are ready to begin implementing their master plan: the release of the Forgotten Gods!

THE ARTIFACTS

To facilitate opening the gate, the Demons seek three items of mystic power. These items are scattered throughout the North American continent. The Demons look for the items in whatever order the PCs expect them to (thus, PCs can intervene at each encounter.)

1. THE POUCH

The first item that the Demons seek is an ancient leather medicine pouch, or more specifically, a peculiar "Y" shaped piece of stone that was found inside this pouch. Archaeologists have theorized that this odd stone item was some odd form of tuning fork and they are close to the truth. This item actually brings the gate to the prison dimension into phase with our reality. Striking the stone upon the altar sets up a resonance vibration in the two columns (see the Serpent Head Island map for details), that aligns the gate with the altar stone. The Wizard can perform this task without the fork, but this ties up half (30 pts.) of his Power Pool.

The pouch and all of its contents (including the fork) are currently on display in the Native American exhibit of a major museum in the GM's campaign.

The Wizard and three selected gang members arrive at the museum shortly after closing time. The Wizard uses a "sleep" spell (4d6 EGO Attack) to subdue guards while the kids attempt to defeat any alarms they encounter. Then the Wizard and his companions proceed to the display, shatter the glass, and the Wizard shifts 40 points of his power pool from EGO attack to a 25" Teleport, 4x Mass, Full Turn to Activate, with 1 Floating Point (a pre-selected location outside of the museum), and escapes, unless PCs intervene. If this occurs, the Wizard tries to grab the fork and escape, leaving the kids behind as a distraction for the PCs. Once outside, he may adjust his Power Pool into a summoning spell which calls forth some shambling horror to menace local innocents, if he feels that the PCs have a chance of catching him.

2. THE CUBE

The second object sought is a cube formed out of rose quartz. This item enhances the possessor's perception (+4 on all PER rolls, and either Danger Sense (not surprised in combat) on 11-, or a +5 on existing Danger Sense, if the possessor already has that Talent). When placed upon the altar, this cube reveals the seal that the ancient Shaman placed over the gate to the prison dimension. (Again, The Wizard does not need this object; however, rendering the gate-seal visible also ties up half (30 pts.) of his Power Pool, leaving him "defenseless" if he has neither the cube nor the fork!)

The cube is currently in the possession of VIPER, at a Research and Design facility in Indiana (operating under the guise of New Generation Technologies, Ltd.). The cube is a central component in an experimental Laser Cannon (4d6 AP RKA, Burnout if Activation roll (11-) Failed, 32 charges, No Range Penalty, OAF, Bulky) that they are developing here.

Psycho, utilizing his Stealth and Shapechange, sneaks into the base and attempts to grab the cube. The other Demons and a selected band of about ten kids wait outside, with the Wizard, who is Mindlinked (via his Power Pool) to Psycho. If all goes well, Psycho enters the lab, disables the scientists, and grabs the cube. At this point, the Wizard teleports in, and the two Demons teleport out, with the cube. Again, The Wizard is perfectly willing to sacrifice the kids to obtain his goals. If PCs interfere here, the result may be a savage three-sided battle.

GMs running this encounter should use the VIPER agents and mansion/base from the *Champions* hardcover book.

3. THE AXE

The final item that the Demons seek is an ancient stone hatchet. This hatchet is used to break the seal that prevents the Forgotten Gods from escaping their prison dimension. The gate seal has 10 DEF and 24 Body. Any magic weapon (including Enforcer's Scythe) will damage the seal. But if a weapon other than the axe is used, the individual attacking the seal suffers damage as if he had struck himself with his own attack!. This axe is also one more reason why the Wizard requires human allies: if a creature that is not a native to this dimension touches it, that creature suffers a 2d6 NND on every Segment of contact! In addition to the above, the hatchet is also a potent weapon (1 ½d6 AP HKA, Affects Desolid, 0 END, Can be Thrown). Unfortunately, the sorcerer that created the hatchet lacked a complete understanding of the forces he was manipulating, and, as a consequence, the hatchet causes minor, improbable inconveniences (2d6 Unluck) to befall its bearer. The hatchet was fabricated during the first rebellion against the Demons, and was used again during the second invasion attempt by an Indian brave.

This axe is currently located at the northern edges of Hudson Bay, buried deep within an ancient Indian burial mound. Its mystical emanations serve as a beacon for any being with magic powers who happens to be near it (GM discretion as to what "near" means in this case). Local Indian mystics know of the axe and its location, but they are content to leave it where it is. (The local Indians have a number of tales concerning the ill luck associated with the weapon.)

Should the PCs seek this item, they locate it at the same time that the Demons do. The Wizard has brought along one street kid to hold the axe for him. The Demons will go out of their way to protect him if a combat breaks out. During the fight, The Wizard holds back, using his Power Pool to maintain his Shapeshift, while the remaining points are used for defenses (Armor or a Force Field; GM choice) and 10 STR TK. He watches carefully for an opportunity to Telekinetically grab the axe. Once he does this (and takes 2d6 NND per Segment!), he gives the axe to the kid, and then concentrates all of his power on getting himself and the child out of the fight; in this situation, even the other Demons are expendable (he can always summon them back later, anyway).

IF THE DEMONS ARE DEFEATED

The only way for the Demons to be defeated before the Final Battle scene is if the Wizard is destroyed or otherwise removed for any length of time from the Earth. If this happens, the Demons plans are ruined, though some of them may still remain free. Each demon responds to such a situation differently.

It is advised that the GM do whatever is required to ensure the freedom of the Wizard until the final battle occurs. (Once the Wizard is defeated, this adventure is over.) If this becomes impossible, the following section outlines possible alternatives, and describes the reactions of the individual demons.

Psycho attempts to avenge the defeat of the Wizard by hunting down the heroes responsible and attempting to kill them one by one. If he accomplishes this (he shouldn't, though he may seem to come close), he then seeks aid in bringing the Wizard back for another attempt at releasing the Forgotten Gods.

Enforcer seeks the aid of anyone that might be able to grant him greater power. This is probably DEMON (or some similar occult organization). While he works with this group, he attempts to manipulate things so that they free either the Forgotten Gods, the Wizard, or both.

Torch attempts to destroy the world with fire (treat as if he was berserk), striking out blindly at anything that moves until he is defeated or banished.

If the Wizard is defeated, Blade will embark upon a killing spree. His first target will be the Fire Demon, whom he despises. Once he has dealt with Torch, Blade will begin choosing targets at random. He will hunt them down, taunt them, and kill them when he tires of them. (He is a cruel demon, after all.)

Unless there is a powerful wizard among the PCs, the Runt immediately surrenders to the PCs, and begs to suffer whatever fate befell the Wizard, for he wishes to be with his master. If a PC is a powerful magician, however, Runt immediately transfers his allegiance to that wizard. He exists solely to be the servant of a powerful magic-user, and relishes this role.

A number of the servants of the Forgotten Gods may have escaped the Great Banishment on Serpent Head, or have been brought to this world since by misguided sorcerers. Some of them (most likely bound to inanimate objects or magically confined somewhere) may still be present on Earth. If the GM desires, some of them may be freed by the Demons, either to replace lost members, increase their numbers, or to slow down the heroes. All such creatures have high EGO scores (18 minimum), at least 10 points of Life Support (usually Self Contained breathing, or a combination of several Safe Environments and Immortality, although any combination is possible), and some form of Vulnerability to magic. The appearance of such creatures should be truly horrific; perhaps a giant, tentacled dragon, or an amorphous green blob covered with innumerable red eyes...

It is possible that at least one of these creatures could perform the gate-opening spell, thus replacing The Wizard as leader of the Demons, if needed.

TO TRAP A DEMON

Ideally, if the Demons have all of the needed artifacts, either the PCs possess a magic-based individual who can develop a plan similar to the one described below (although a few other possibilities are presented), or they will attempt to locate an NPC who does. The following option is included only for use if the PCs do not or can not use any of the above options, and fail to develop a plan of their own.

Sometime during the Scavenger Hunt episode (preferably right after the Demons have found the last artifact), a mysterious figure manifests itself in the presence of several of the heroes.

This figure wears the costume of a Morbane, but lacks the traditional accoutrements of his kind. This figure introduces himself as Lord Thorne, a member of DEMON's Inner Circle.

Thorne claims that he has come to the PCs because he has discovered that there are real, hostile demons rampaging about the world. He fears that they intend to release a group of entities whose existence is known only to the most knowledgeable students of the occult (the Forgotten Gods).

Thorne fears that the release of these monsters would cause the destruction of all life on Earth, something that neither he nor the heroes wants. However, Thorne has a plan to stop them: he has knowledge of a spell that he believes will turn the ritual of the Demons into a powerful trap. However, he needs someone to keep him safe while he casts it, since the spell can only be cast while the Demons are trying to open the gate and it requires his full concentration.

Of all the Inner Circle members, only Thorne has recognized the danger. The others believe that the Forgotten Gods will be on friendly terms with them, but Thorne is a scholar of the ancient gods and he knows the truth: that DEMON will be consumed just like the rest of the world. For this reason, he is unable to obtain the aid he needs from DEMON, and must seek it elsewhere. As the PCs possess first hand knowledge of the Demons (having encountered them recently), they are the most logical choice.

He fears that time is short, and must have their answer immediately — will they help him, or must he look elsewhere?

If the PCs seem to doubt his good intentions, he repeatedly approaches them with information on the Demons, warning the PCs of where the Demons probably intend to strike next, offering them weapons to use against the Demons, etc. If the PCs find sorcerous assistance elsewhere, he leaves them alone; otherwise, he continually pesters them until they accept his aid or go into the final battle unassisted.

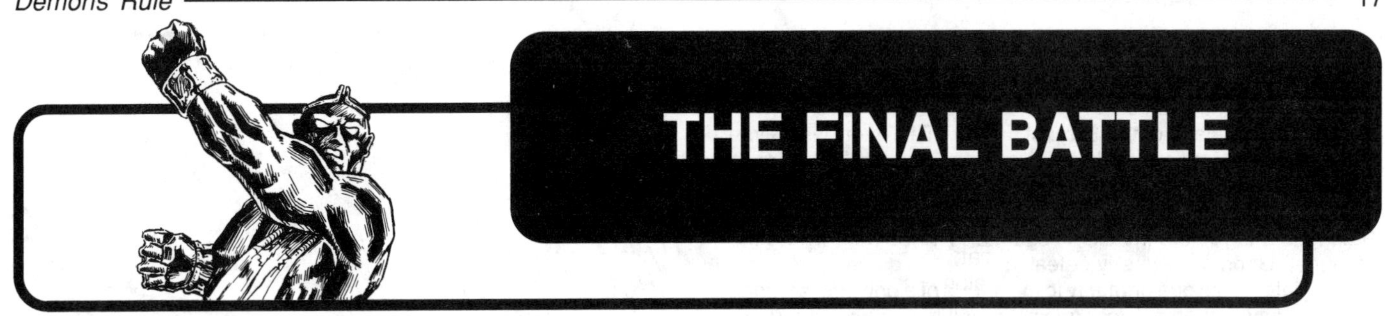

THE FINAL BATTLE

By now, the characters should have noticed the connection between the late author Howard Pickman and the Demons. PCs examining his writings notice that many of his stories are set in Massachusetts, and that a vast majority of these stories involve Lake Perigannsett and the neighboring community of Dunham, the city that contains Pickman's Alma Mater. This information, possibly coupled with other clues or a successful Deduction roll, indicates that Lake Perigannsett has a strong connection to the Demons.

Armed with the information they have obtained through research, a plan of some sort, and possibly the aid of a supervillain or magic-based NPC, the PCs head for Serpent Head Island for a final confrontation with the Demons.

During this encounter, the PCs will face the Demons one last time. The stakes: the fate of the world. If the Heroes do not manage to stop the Demons from completing their ritual, they will summon the Forgotten Gods, humanity will be enslaved and the world will become a wasteland of death and destruction. Somehow, the heroes must find a way to defeat the Demons and banish them from the Earth forever.

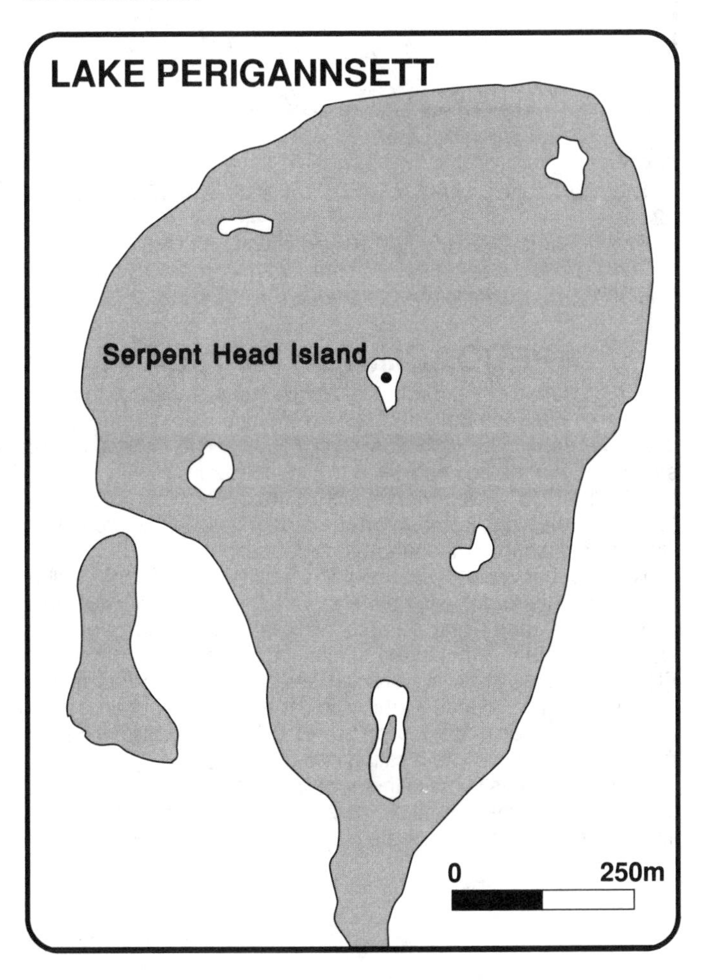

The Demons may be banished in a number of ways. If one of the PCs is a spell user, he could cast a spell capable of forcing the Demon's back through the gate. If none of the PCs are mages, then the GM could introduce an NPC (perhaps Lord Thorn) to aid the heroes.

If the GM (or the players) prefers a more "violent" resolution (albeit one that does not require them to obtain outside assistance), perhaps a Force Wall, Force Field, or some derivative of TK could be used to prevent the demons on the other side of the gate from coming through, while strong heroes could physically hurl those Demons here across to the other side. Other options along these lines are possible, and inventive players may stumble upon even more solutions to this problem; if they do, and this plan sounds reasonable, let it work!

If the PCs are extremely powerful, the following option may be used: The spell that the Wizard knows only summons the Lord of the Void to this realm. If this option is used, the Lord of the Void is the only being who possesses enough power to open the gate fully, and he intends to do so once he arrives in this world. In this case, the PCs arrive on the island just as the Demons finish their spell, and they must face both the Demons and the Lord of the Void! (Stats for the Lord of the Void are not given with this adventure but it is suggested that he be truly frightening.)

LAKE PERIGANNSETT & SERPENT HEAD ISLAND

The large map of the area around Serpent Head is scaled so that every hex is 24 meters across. This map shows the location of the island and several other small islands in the lake. To the north of the lake, on the land containing the smaller "Ox bow" lake, is the Lake Perigannsett Country Club, complete with a golf course, tennis courts, etc. Several small groups of people are out there, enjoying these facilities at any given time, although bad weather drives a majority of them indoors. To the south and east are two small towns that are about fifteen years out of date; many of the locals spend their time hunting, fishing, and laughing at those who are dependant on "modern conveniences."

To the west, further down the Perigannsett River, is the college town of Dunham. Dunham University is a small, provincial college with one of the world's most renowned parapsychological investigation facilities (featured about once a month in any number of the many tabloids available at grocery stores across the country). The college library contains books that may provide information on the Forgotten Gods and the history of the island, if the GM so desires. Other details for these areas are left to the GM to determine as needed.

HISTORY

The modern name for the island (Serpent Head) is actually due to an error in translation of the name that the natives gave it, which meant literally "Island of the Serpent Father." This name was given to the island because local legends claimed that the Father of all Serpents resided in a complex beneath the island.

It was during a ritual to appease this deity that the accident leading to the Second Invasion began, and it was here where the Forgotten Gods were utterly defeated.

This defeat was due primarily to the efforts of a powerful shaman and the army that he brought against these monsters. During this battle, the Shaman managed to use his own "spirit powers" to open a gate to an abandoned dimension, and another of the braves present, one wielding the mystic axe described above, chased the Forgotten Gods through. Once they were through, the Shaman used a crystal cube (the rose quartz cube) as a focus to create an invisible barrier that would seal off the formerly vacant dimension forever. This done, he channeled his powers through a stone fork, and forced the gate "out of phase" with the rest of our reality.

This completed, he summoned and bound two elemental spirits into stone pillars on the island, to prevent anyone from releasing the creatures imprisoned there.

Today the island stands deserted; not even the birds and fish that are so plentiful elsewhere on the lake come near it. Although the local fisher-folk no longer believe that demons or evil spirits live on the island, they stay clear of it. Something about it just makes them nervous...

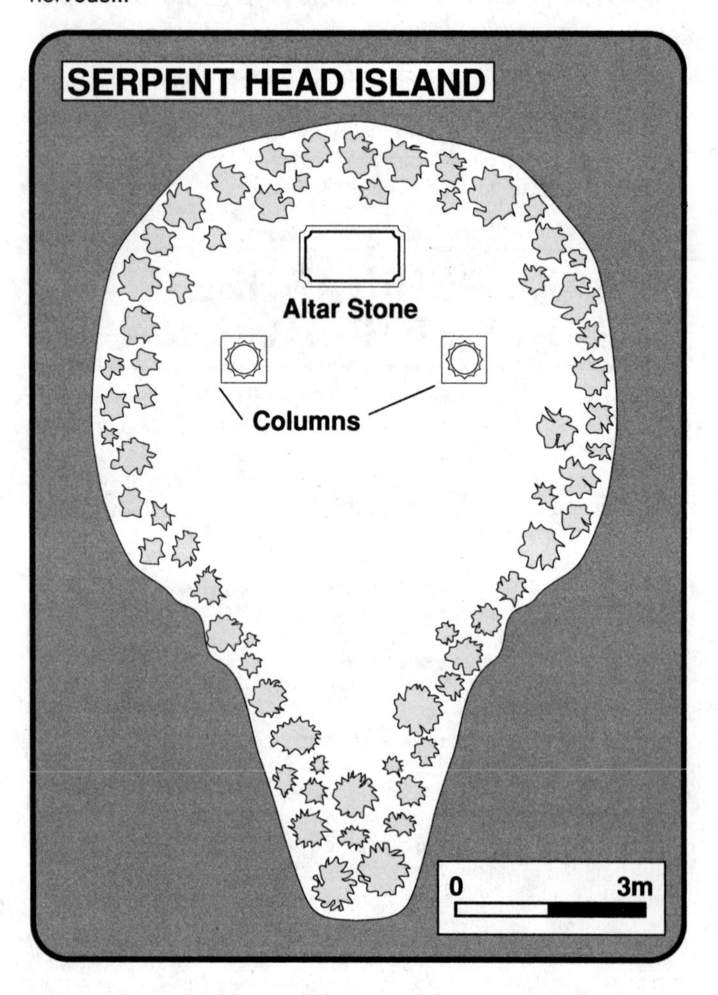

KEY

The Altar Stone is nearly four tons of granite. It has DEF 6, BODY 12.

Each Pillar is DEF 6 BODY 10 and weighs 800 kg.

There are two sizes of trees on the island. Large ones have DEF 5, BODY 8, and smaller ones have DEF 4, BODY 5.

APPROACHING THE ISLAND

The presence of the Elemental Spirits makes it difficult to reach the island. First, the Spirits impair the ability of others to reach the island by sea or air (8d6 Drain vs. Flight and Swimming), and second, they make it impossible to Teleport to the island, as they simply "bounce" Teleporters back to their points of departure. (Consider the Island to be surrounded by a 1 DEF Force Wall, Double Hardened, Transparent to All Attacks.)

Thus, reaching the island should be a difficult but not impossible task. The Wizard, for example, reaches the island by going to a nearby island and using a Force Wall as a bridge; creative PCs should be able to formulate a similar plan. If the PCs have read Pickman's books, they might remember that the island was used in one of Pickman's stories. In this book, the cultists reached the isle by constructing an underground tunnel. If the PCs look for a tunnel, they will have no trouble locating one.

If the GM wishes to make this approach difficult, the tunnel could be inhabited by many snakes, as Indian legends about the island imply. The tunnel exits beneath one of the columns (GM choice as to which one).

CLIMAX

GATE CRASHING

As indicated in the descriptions of the artifacts, the seal on the gate has 10 DEF and 24 Body. Nonmagical weapons can't damage the seal at all and magical weapons other than the axe will cause the user to take damage as well. Roll normally each phase for the kid to hit and damage the seal. (He has a 12- roll to hit the gate, and does 2d6 AP HKA with the axe.) The gate must be opened for the banishment spell (if one is being used) to be effective. The casting of the Banishment spell requires one full turn (during which the caster must remain undamaged.)

MOTHER NATURE STIRS THE POT

Now, as if all of this were not enough, there is one more detail to be concerned about: Nature. The opening of a large gate causes a disruption of the environment.

This initially causes some minor atmospheric disturbances (Segments one through three during the first round of combat), such as lightning flares in the sky (on an 8- roll, any one using a metallic focus may be struck by a lightening bolt, with damage based upon how well grounded that character is. For particulars, see *Champions* , pg. S44.

After Segment 3, however, the winds in the area pick up, acting as a TK Explosion, that loses 1 DC per 24" (Thus each area affected is represented by one hex on the large map of lake Perigannsett and its surroundings.) Initially, this is only 5 STR Telekinesis, but every 3 segments, this increases by 5 STR, until it reaches a maximum STR of 60. When the battle is over, the winds fade at the same rate that it built up. As the wind's strength increases, so do the chances for normals to become imperiled. This may provide Thorne (or a similarly greedy magic-based NPC, if one is present) with an opportunity to grab the artifacts and flee, if the PCs notice the damage being done to the area before they pay him any real attention. Just to make things more interesting, there may be any number of boats on the lake at any given time.

RUNNING THE BATTLE

When the PCs arrive, most of the Demons head out to "greet" them. The Wizard, however, is engaged in the attempt to open the gate, and will not be directly in the battle.

Because the Wizard is not there to lead them, chances are slim that the Demons will use teamwork, and most will revert to their preferred means of battle. This means that Blade will single out one hero and attempts to kill him, Torch strikes at whatever targets suit his fancy (probably alternating frequently, and occasionally setting fire to trees), Enforcer stands guard over the Wizard (fearing that the Wizard's defences are not sufficient) until the gate is opened, and Psycho employs his Shapechange powers and Stealth skills to scout out the heroes so that he can slay any spell casters among them.

Expecting the PCs to interfere, The Wizard has also brought along a number of the street kids. These are the most loyal ones that he could find, and have been given the best equipment that he could locate (the GM should select armor and weapons as appropriate, from the charts on pgs. 199-200 of *Champions*). These kids already know the true nature of their "bosses" and either do not mind or are so fully under the Demon's control that they don't care. There are three kids for each PC present, in addition to the kid with the axe.

When a fight breaks out, one third of the youths remain behind with Enforcer to protect the Wizard, while the others seek cover within the trees, so that they may strike at the heroes from concealment. Unlike the Demons, these kids may employ some degree of teamwork (all have fought together before, and are therefore able to coordinate attacks).

Note that if the Demons are banished, or otherwise forced through the gate, there is nothing to prevent them from returning, unless the PCs come up with some method of sealing off the gate. Force Walls may be used, as can Telekinesis, a one-hex Entangle, or some similar Power. Observant PCs should notice that the altar stone is about the right size for this, assuming one of them can lift it.

Of course, few of these seals are permanent. To finish the task, the PCs will have to find some way of actually closing or banishing the sealed gate. Striking the Fork against either of the pillars may send the portal slowly out of phase (GM option), possibly trapping some nameless horror seeking to escape at the last minute. Or a PC (or NPC) wizard could create a simple spell to seal the portal off, but the PCs will have to hold back demons that seek to come out until the spell is in completed...

Remember, this fight is an all out battle on all sides, with no holds barred and the fate of the world hanging in the balance. It is the GMs task to squeeze as much tension and drama out of it as possible.

AFTERMATH

IF THE HEROES WON

After the battle, everything slowly returns to normal. The PCs have triumphed over the Demons, but there is still a mess to clean up. The local storms caused by the gate's opening have flooded various areas and the winds have caused a great deal of property damage. The PCs should have plenty to do with helping repair the damage and rescue stranded victims. Of course, the PCs must also figure out what they're going to do with the brainwashed street kids.

IF THE HEROES LOST

Things are pretty grim. This probably means that the Demons were successful in summoning the Forgotten Gods and the world is in big trouble. The GM has two options here.

The first is to have something go wrong with the summoning ritual which would give the PCs another chance to stop the Demons. Perhaps one of the artifacts is a fake, or something is wrong with the spell. GMs should be careful about using this solution as it gives the PCs the idea that no matter what they do wrong, they will always be given a second chance.

The Second option is to drastically alter the campaign setting and say that the Demons were successful. This would mean the the Forgotten Gods were summoned to Earth. (These creatures should be very large and powerful, built on about 1200 points.) The PCs must now fight a long and hard battle against the new invaders. Appropriate source material for such a campaign would include *Invasions: Target Earth* and Horror World from *Champions in 3-D*.

EXPERIENCE

The total experience that should be awarded for this adventure may vary from campaign to campaign, but a base of four or five points is suggested. Characters were in a long involved scenario (2pts), that probably ran for more than one session (+1pt), where the PCs had to solve mysteries(+1pt). Additionally, if a player runs one (or more) of the NPCs in the Danger in the Streets section, and that player handles the NPC(s) well (GM discretion), his character may be awarded an additional experience point.

SPIN OFFS

Perhaps things are not quite over yet. The observant GM will see numerous "loose ends" hanging about in this set of episodes. Some of these are listed below, along with a number of other, not-so-obvious, "campaign hooks." These hooks have been left relatively vague so that the GM has a springboard to work from, but is otherwise unrestrained.

1. The organized street gangs may remain organized even after the Demons are defeated. Reasons for this could be as simple as the gangs enjoying the power gained by cooperation, to something as complex as some supervillain or villainous organization like DEMON or VIPER using the gangs as some kind of decoy or private army.

2. One or more of the Demons may have escaped the Final Battle. If this occurs, see the section *If the Demons are Defeated.*

3. The Earth of the Demons' origin might not be the PCs' Earth, but a parallel world instead. This opens up many possibilities, if the demons are banished as described in the concluding chapter:

3a. Perhaps the banishment spell not only imprisoned the Demons, but also sent the PCs to the alternate Earth as well. On this world, perhaps science never developed (heating and cooking are done via enslaved Fire Elementals, Cross-oceanic transport is done with the aid of Water Elementals, the Olympics are a Magic Competition, or perhaps it followed a history identical to that the PCs know, except that there are no superheroes or villains, or perhaps the PCs have evil analogs here...The possibilities are virtually endless! (See *Champions in 3-D* for appropriate source material.)

3b. The banishment spell could accidentally bring something through from this other world (perhaps an enraged elemental, an evil analog to a PC, someone's vacationing grandmother, or anything else the GM's fiendish mind can come up with). 3a and 3b need not be mutually exclusive...

4. One of the gang members may have learned some magic or could have been altered by the Wizard and thus could become a supervillain.

5. If one of the heroes is captured by the Demons, it is possible that he became possessed by the Lord of the Void or another of The Forgotten Gods (see the "Possession Set" under The Wizard's Powers). If an NPC or PC became a vessel for one of these creatures, his body has probably been destroyed, but what of the life-force, or soul? Perhaps it is in some other realm, or perhaps it is held by one of the Forgotten Gods, and is in the prison dimension with them! This could lead to a foray into the prison dimension, and perhaps a re-match with the Demons, or perhaps encounters with worse terrors. In addition, if the soul is regained, what will it be put in? The original body is probably gone, so something else will have to be used instead.

6. The banishment spell could also send the PCs to the prison dimension. For this and #5, above, this dimension was once entirely vacant, and has about ½ the land mass of the Earth, though this is not contiguous, nor are all of its areas on one dimensional plane. Now, picture this area filled with super powered or demonic villains expelled from numerous dimensions for their crimes, each with a team of friends or flunkies and you have a pretty good idea of what this domain is like.

NPCS

THE WIZARD (MORGALIS)

Val	Char	Cost	100+	Disadvantages
25	STR	15	20	1 ½x STUN, BODY from Magic
24	DEX	42	20	Accidental Change to true form when struck, 11-
23	CON	26	20	Berserk after taking body, 14-,14-
10	BODY	0	20	Serves the Forgotten Gods
23	INT	13	15	Ruthless, vicious
21	EGO	22	15	Needs to be in charge
33	PRE	23	5	No Legs in true form
10	COM	0	20	Distinctive Features: No legs, small head, three arms
15	PD	10	15	Hunted by DEMON 8-
15	ED	10	10	Hunted by the Circle 8-
6	SPD	26	15	Secret ID (Street punk known only as "Wiz" or "The Wizard")
10	REC	0	172	Demon Bonus
60	END	7		
45	STUN	10		

Cost	Power	END
90	60 point. Variable Power Pool (Magic) Common Power Sets	
	"Wizard" Set 1: (Note: This and the other "Wizard Set" are used only when the Wizard is in his human guise)	
(15)	Disguise Spell: Shapeshift to Human Form, 0 END	0
(45)	Shield Spell: Force Field (+ 15 PD, 15 ED), Invisible to Sight.	4
	"Wizard" Set 2:	
(15)	Disguise Spell: Shapeshift to Human Form, 0 END	0
(15)	Phantom Armor: Armor (+ 8 PD, 7 ED), Extra Time: Full Phase	
(30)	Domination: 12d6 Mind Control, No Range, Extra Time: Full Phase	6
	Battle Set:	
(35)	Barrier of Force: Force Field (+ 17 PD, 18 ED)	3
(12)	Death Touch: Penetrating Effect on HKA	
(13)	Protective Servant: Missile Deflection vs. All attacks, Linked to Shield Spell	
	Standard Set:	
(35)	Teleport Spell: 15" Teleport, 1 Floating Point	3
(25)	Cloak Of Obscurement: Invisibility vs Normal, UV Vision	2
	"Possession" Set: (Used to prepare a victim to Host a Demon, Only if Need for Hosts Option (see GM Background) used, or an opportunity to summon the Lord of the Void arises.)	
(17)	Indoctrinate: 2d6 Major Transformation, Human to Limited Group (Demon Host), Cumulative, Full Turn to Activate, No Range, only works at Night. Victim Becomes "Loyal to The Wizard", Vulnerable to Magic (2x STUN Hunted by the Circle (11-), but gains Multiform to a Demon. Reversed by successful (GM Discretion as to what that means) expulsion	5
(30)	Hold Victim: 3d6, 3 DEF Entangle, Invisible to Sight, Transparent to Attacks, No Range, Requires Gestures, Incantation to activate	6
(13)	Weaken: 2d6 Characteristic Drain vs. STR, Linked to Hold Victim Spell	2
25	1 ½d6 HKA (3d6 +1 w/STR): Claws	+2
24	Life Support: Breathing Self Contained, Does not Age, needs not eat or excrete Immune to High Pressure, Immune to Intense Heat/Cold	
51	17" Flight, 0 End Cost	0
10	1 BODY Regeneration	
5	Damage Resistance (5 PD/5 ED)	
5	Extra Limb: Third Arm	
3	Ambidexterity	
15	Magic Skill 20-	
3	Oratory 16-	
3	Persuasion 16-	
3	Tactics 15-	
2	KS: Dimensional Knowledge 11-	
4	1 Language, As a Native (That of Summoner)	

OCV: 7; **DCV:** 7; **ECV:** 7; **Phases:** 2,4,6,8,10,12

Costs:	Chars		Powers		Total		Disadv		Base
	204	+	243	=	447	=	347	+	100

Background: The entity known as Morgalis was created by the Lord of the Void out of the raw material of Chaos. Finding his home dimension boring, Morgalis took to wandering at an early age. He occasionally returned to his creator, out of a sense of obligation, but spent increasingly more time away from "home".

During these trips, Morgalis explored many dimensions, conquering some for his master, and simply observing others. The more he travelled, the more powerful he began to feel. In his home dimension, the only other sentient creature was his master, the Lord of the Void; a vast creature that made the Wizard's power seem totally insignificant. In other dimensions, the inhabitants had no magic at all... no power of any kind. Compared to these creatures, the Wizard was like a god.

By the time Morgalis came across a world of bipedal creatures that would one day be known as Earth, he felt that nothing could stand in his way. Yet the dimension's inhabitants overcame Morgalis and banished him back to the Void from which he was born.

Infuriated, Morgalis made many more attempts to conquer the Earth, each one being thwarted by some human magician, one of whom set up a special magical barrier to prevent Morgalis and his kind from returning without being asked back by a native to the mortal plane. Eventually, Earth became more then just another dimension to be conquered — It became Morgalis' bane. Every time he tried to conquer the world, he was defeated. Now he has been resummoned to Earth and he is through toying with humans. He intends to conquer the Earth or die trying.

Distinctive Quote: "You cannot even begin to comprehend what you are up against!"

Personality: While the Wizard is no coward, he could easily be perceived as one. He realizes that he is the only one of his group that can summon the other Demons back to the Earth and he is the only one who can cast the spell to re-open the door to the Limbo where his masters are imprisoned, so he protects himself accordingly. The Wizard is a cruel, shrewd, calculating creature. If he has any socially redeeming qualities (aside from his faithfulness to the so-called Forgotten Gods), he hides them well. To The Wizard, all humans are expendable, as are his allies. He cares only for himself and his dark masters.

Powers/Tactics: Being a demon, The Wizard has a number of strange abilities. He possesses three arms, all of which end in three short, fully-opposable, razor-sharp digits, and no legs. In his natural form, his lower body is surrounded by a small whirlwind that allows him to fly. The Wizard is also a trained sorcerer, possessing an almost infinite variety of spells as well. This is reflected by his Power Pool. Some examples of common spell sets are described among his Powers; other sets may be created, along these lines. (Other ideas for Spells may be found in *Fantasy Hero* and the *Fantasy Hero Companion.*)

The Wizard always hangs in the back during a fight, and flees if it seems that his side may lose. He also tries to keep his demonic nature secret as long as possible (masquerading as a "mere sorcerer" until he has to show his true nature). If not in his true shape, he employs simple weapons (or spell-generated copies, perhaps with advantages or a few extra dice damage added in), and attempts to isolate single heroes for "brainwashing" (via Mind Control or perhaps Indoctrination)

In his true form, he usually attempts to shred enemies with his talons, perhaps using his power pool to enhance them. If injured, he tries to flee.

Appearance: In his disguise as the "Wizard," Morgalis appears to be a human male 6' tall, slender, and in his early twenties. His hair is red-blond and his face is very angular. In his natural state, the Wizard looks more like a turnip than a man; his lower body ends in a legless, rounded cone, and three arms project about the rim at the broad top. Above these arms is his head, slightly smaller than that of a man. Two huge, black-irised eyes (with glowing blue pupils) are the most prominent features of his head. His mouth (the only visible feature aside from the eyes) is about the size of a human's, but has no lips and is lined with rows of jagged teeth. His entire body is a tan color, except as noted previously and his claws, which are a metallic gray. His lower body is supported on a whirlwind while he is conscious.

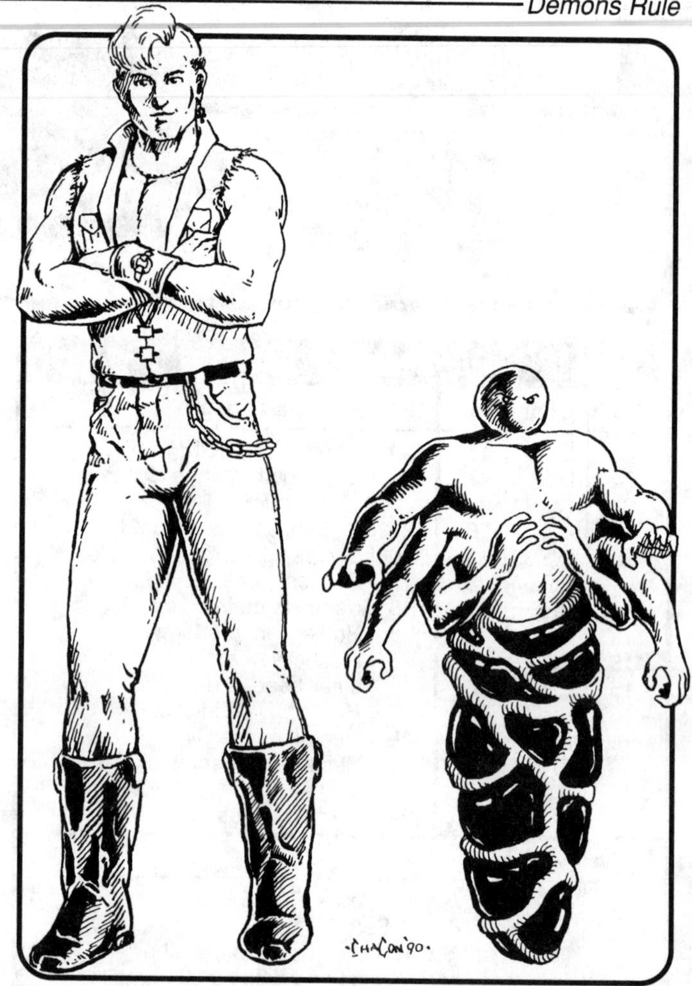

TORCH (CONFLAR)

Val	Char	Cost	100+	Disadvantages
9	STR	-1	20	2x STUN from Cold Based Attacks
26	DEX	47	10	2x STUN, BODY from Cold Iron
27	CON	36	25	Berserk when restrained or entangled, 14-, 11-
13	BODY	6	20	Overconfident
13	INT	3	15	Irrational love of fire
15	EGO	10	15	Irrationally loyal to the Wizard
13	PRE	3	20	Distinctive Features: Human bathed in flames
10	COM	0	10	Reputation, arsonist 11-
5	PD	3	10	Hunted by the Circle 8-
5	ED	-1	15	Hunted by DEMON 8-
6	SPD	24	20	Hunted by Police 14-
10	REC	4	15	Secret ID
60	END	2	113	Demon Bonus
40	STUN	8		

Cost	Power	END
20	EC — Demonfire	
a - 20	1d6+1 RKA Damage Shield, 0 END	0
b - 20	Force Field (+ 20 PD, 20 ED), 0 END, Linked to Damage Shield	0
c - 20	20" Flight	4
60	Multipower (60 points, Demon Fire)	
6 u	8d6 AP EB	6
11 m	3d6 RKA, ½ END	2
6 u	8d6 EB, Affects Desolidified	6
10 m	10d6 EB	5
25	1 ½d6 HKA	2
25	Shapeshift to Any Humanoid Form, ½ Endurance	
10	1 BODY Regeneration	
24	Life Support: Self Contained Breathing, Doesn't Age, No Need to Eat or Excrete, Immune to Pressure & Extreme Heat	
3	Demolitions 11-	
4	Language: That of summoner, as Native	

OCV: 9; **DCV:** 9; **ECV:** 5; **Phase:** 2,4,6,8,10,12

Costs:	Chars		Powers		Total		Disadv		Base
	144	+	264	=	408	=	308	+	100

Background: Deep within the bowels of the universe there is a great realm of burning fire. This is the home of the fire elementals and the original birthplace of Conflar. Most fire elementals never leave their home dimension, but Conflar was different. Much like the Wizard, Conflar had a wanderlust that could not be controlled. When the Wizard summoned an elemental from the plane of fire, Conflar gladly answered.

When Conflar arrived on Earth, the Wizard used his dark sorcery to taint Conflar's soul and transform him from an elemental into a Fire Demon. The Wizard granted him a True Name (most demons only receive True Names after developing a unique ability or finding a unique magic item, permitting them to gain power over their brethren) and gave him a place of importance by his side. Ever since that time, Torch has been loyal to the Wizard, but not necessarily to the Forgotten Gods. When the Wizard originally attempted to enslave the Earth, Torch was by his side. Now, thousands of years and a few failures later, Torch is still there by his master's side.

Distinctive Quote: "Pretty Fire. Hee, hee, hee!"

Personality: Torch is a born pyromaniac. In the middle of a fire, he appears to act like a child in a candy store. He is probably the most dangerous and "immature" (if such a term can apply to a demon) of all the Demons, and he is most certainly the most volatile. He is also the least predictable; essentially his personality mirrors his beloved flame. Torch is overconfident and he feels that between his abilities and his master's sorcery, the Demons are an unbeatable team.

Powers/Tactics: As with all Fire Demons, Torch can manipulate "Demonfire," magical flames that originate outside of his body. When he uses his powers, he is actually opening a conduit to his native plane. Cold iron causes some feedback along this conduit, and thus causes him great pain. Torch's flames are usually a red-violet color, although he can change their colors at will. His flight leaves a trail of "phantom fire," fire that seems real, but cannot affect anything on the mortal realm (some supernatural creatures and magic based characters may feel some pain if they cross this trail, at the GM's option). Torch enjoys "lighting up," and claims to be a mutant until his true nature is made obvious. He is visibly impressed by any fire based supers, and may pause to talk "shop" with them, if given a chance.

Torch darts about the battlefield, rarely striking the same foe more than once in succession, unless ordered to do so. He usually employs his RKA or the 10d6 blast, unless a need for one of the other attacks arises, and he employs none of his attacks unless both force field and his damage shield are active (whether or not this is personal choice or a restriction on his powers is unknown). He tends to giggle a lot in battle, and often attacks inanimate objects (unless ordered not to), just to start a "lovely fire."

Appearance: In his demonic form, Torch appears to be a slender human male literally bathed in flames. His legs are not visible; Torch's torso ends in a column of fire. In his human form, Conflar appears to be a well-built man with a deep tan, red hair, and hazel eyes. He is the most human-looking of the Demons. He usually wears a T-shirt (advertising the Def Leppard "Pyromania" tour), dark jeans, and red cowboy boots.

BLADE (SHARGAAS)				
Val	**Char**	**Cost**	**100+**	**Disadvantages**
23	STR	13	20	1 ½ STUN, BODY from Fire
26	DEX	48	20	Berserk when foes using fire,
28	CON	36		11-, 11-
14	BODY	8	15	Enjoys killing
18	INT	8	15	Cowardly
18	EGO	16	5	1d6/Phase from contact with
18	PRE	8		Cold Iron
6	COM	-2	20	Distinctive Features: Humanoid
5	PD	0		with protruding spikes
7	ED	1	10	Hunted by the Circle, 8-
5	SPD	14	10	Hunted by DEMON, 8-
11	REC	0	15	Hunted by Police, 14-
56	END	0	15	Secret ID (Blade)
40	STUN	0	130	Demon Bonus

Cost	Power	END
22	EC — Ice Powers	
a - 28	1d6+1 AP HKA, usable at range, 0 END, OIF Ice Shards	0(+1)
b - 23	3d6 NND Damage Shield (Intense Cold), 0 END	0
c - 23	4 ½d6 Entanglement, Ice bonds	4
d - 28	10d6 EB: Ice bolt	5
e - 23	12 rPD/18 rED Armor , Icy coating	
24	Life Support: Self Contained Breathing, No Need to Eat or Excrete, Immune to extreme Pressure & cold, Does not Age	
25	Shapeshift to Any Humanoid, ½ END	1
10	1 BODY Regeneration	
1	FAM: Knives	
3	Weaponsmith: Knives 11-	
15	3 Levels with all knives	

OCV: 9; **DCV:** 9; **ECV:** 6; **Phases:** 2,4,6,7,9,11,12

Costs:	Chars		Powers		Total		Disadv		Base
	150	+	225	=	375	=	275	+	100

Background: Just as there is an Elemental Plane of Fire, somewhere in the universe there is a plane full of icy crags and cold air: the Elemental Plane of Ice. Once, it was home to a proud race of Ice Elementals. Then dissension broke out, and some powerful Ice Elementals sought to take control of the realm. This caused a long and bloody war that left all but a few of the creatures dead.

One of these survivors was Shargaas. A coward at heart, Shargaas desperately wished to leave his shattered home plane. This was when he met with the Extra-Dimensional demon, Morgalis. The Demon agreed to take the Ice Elemental with him if he promised him eternal service. Shargaas agreed and Morgalis' evil tainted him, transforming him into an Ice Demon.

Shargaas, sometimes known as Blade (the Wizard suggested the name after noticing the demon's love of sharp objects), has fought alongside Morgalis during his first two attempts to take Earth. He was one of the first demons to fall during the first invasion, and he fared no better during the second. However, he has made an oath, and he must stick to it. He is determined to make this invasion a success.

Distinctive Quote: "Oh. I'm sorry. I didn't know that you wanted them alive..."

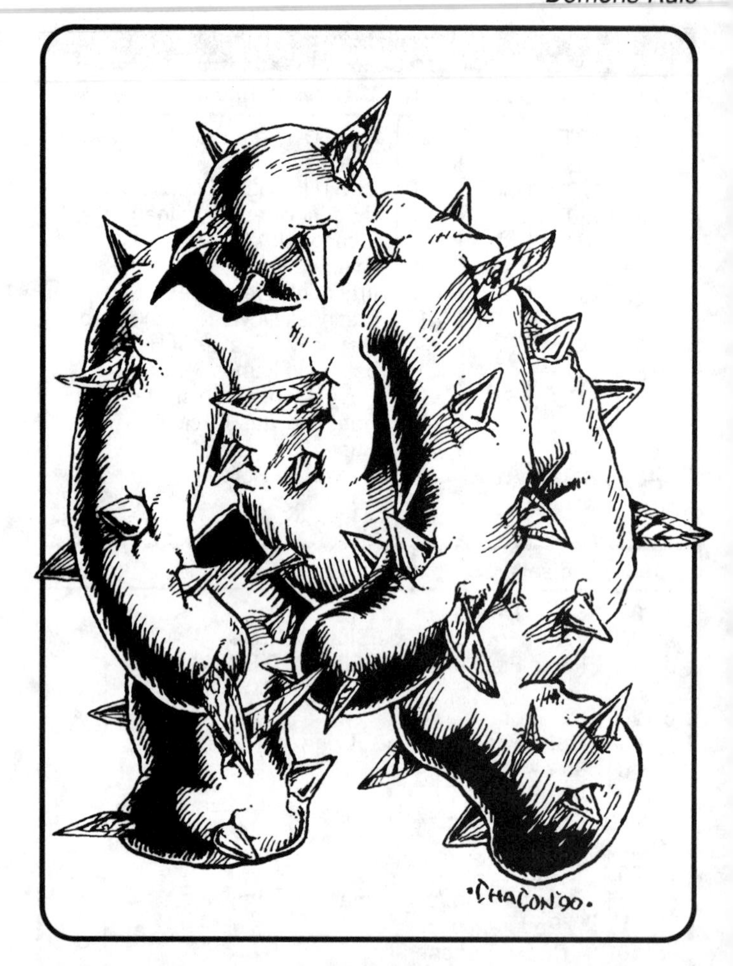

Personality: Blade (Shargaas' current name) is primarily motivated by fear. He is a bully and a coward. As long as he is sure that he can beat his opponent, Blade is unrelenting and sadistic. Should his opponent actually hurt him, however, Shargaas will go on the defensive and attempt to escape. He rarely speaks at all, and then usually only to grumble. The only thing that really makes him happy is cutting up living beings and watching the blood drain out — slowly. Blade loves to use edged weapons. Blade hates the Fire demon, Torch, both because the Wizard favors him and because the Fire Demon is capable of hurting him.

Powers/Tactics: Blade comes from a frozen realm, and his body forms a conduit to that plane. Through this channel, Blade can summon cold and ice from his home plane. He can shape this Ice into armor, ice bolts, and small glaciers (useful for entangling opponents.) Being an Ice Demon, intense heat causes Blade a great deal of pain and makes him very uncomfortable, making his already nasty temper even nastier. Cold Iron, a notoriously anti-magical metal, causes some feedback through the extra-dimensional conduit which injures the Demon. Blade — like all Frost Demons — has amazingly fast reflexes.

Blade always enters combat reluctantly, singles out one opponent, and attacks that opponent until either he falls or the demon takes damage from another enemy. Blade frequently strikes downed foes when a reasonable chance to do so presents itself. Blade knows no mercy.

Appearance: Blade, in his normal (demonic) form appears as a pale humanoid of medium height and build with spikes jutting through its skin in numerous places. As a human he is pale, has platinum-blond hair, and is also still extremely tall and thin, though not as much so as in his demonic form. He wears a black leather jacket and wields a perfectly balanced "Bowie" knife. He also wears leather slacks and boots, and a leather cap (actually a Greek sailor's cap).

PSYCHO (ZOLIGAHR)

Val	Char	Cost	100+	Disadvantages
25	STR	15	20	2x STUN from Magic
30	DEX	60	15	2x STUN, 1 ½x BODY from Cold Iron
23	CON	26	20	Berserk at the sight of blood, 11-, 11-
11	BODY	2	15	Loyal to the Wizard
18	INT	8	15	Killer
18	EGO	16	20	Distinctive Features: Animal features, smell of blood
18	PRE	8	5	Distinctive Features: Aura of fear
8	COM	-1	10	Hunted by the Circle 8-
20	PD	15	10	Hunted by DEMON 8-
10	ED	5	20	Hunted by Police 14-
7	SPD	30	155	Demon Bonus
10	REC	0		
46	END	0		
40	STUN	4		

Cost	Power	END
52	2d6 AP HKA, ½ END, (3d6 w/STR), Jaws	2(3)
30	Shapeshift to Human or Predatory Animal, 0 END	0
15	Multipower (30 points), Linked with Shapeshift, Only as appropriate for form assumed	
1 u	20 pts Growth, 0 END	0
1 u	20 pts Shrinking, 0 END	0
10	10" flight, OAF Wings	1
27	Life Support: Breathing Self Contained, Does Not Age, Immune to Disease, Pressure and Temperature Extremes, No Need to Eat or Excrete	
10	1 BODY Regeneration	
6	½ END on STR	1
10	Tracking Scent	
5	UV Vision	
4	+2 Hearing	
5	Discriminatory Smell	
6	+2 with all Senses	
3, 3, 3	Acrobatics, Breakfall, Climbing (all 15-)	
9, 9, 5	Mimicry, Shadowing, Concealment (all 14-)	
3	Stealth 15-	

OCV: 10; **DCV:** 10; **ECV:** 6; **Phase:** 2,4,6,7,9,11,12

Costs:	Chars		Powers		Total		Disadv		Base
	188	+	217	=	405	=	305	+	100

Background: The Demon hounds of Prince Thk'Cholla are renowned as being the among the best hunters in the multiverse. Their mastery of stealth, tracking, and killing is indisputable, as is their loyalty. Free will had never been heard of in a demon hound — until Zoligahr.

While hunting imps in the nether realms, the Prince refused Zoligahr a kill. Infuriated at being denied the opportunity to destroy something, Zoligahr attacked his master in a blind rage. After beating the hound down, Thk'Cholla decided to execute him.

Morgalis, seeking a band of fierce demons to lead the original assault on Earth, heard of Zoligahr and came to his aid. Morgalis offered the Prince an ancient artifact in return for the rabid demon hound. Thk'Cholla accepted, and Morgalis had added another member to his ranks.

Today, Zohligar is known as Psycho (because of his rabid lust for death). The Demon hound still serves Morgalis and the two demons are as close to friendship as is possible for such creatures.

Distinctive Quote: "The Thrill of the Hunt, the Joy of the Kill. It is for this that I exist."

Personality: Psycho, a hunter at heart, enjoys stalking prey for as long as possible, and then pouncing on it for a quick kill. Psycho is cruel, cunning, and efficient at everything he does. He is loyal to the Wizard and usually obeys the Demon Lord's directives. However, his animalistic tendencies often cause him to go off on his own and hunt. Psycho dislikes mass battles, preferring one-on-one combat: predator and prey.

Powers/Tactics: Psycho was constructed out of the vast void known as Chaos by the Demon Prince Thk'Cholla. He was made to be a predator... a killer. As such, Zoligahr is very well equipped for his job. Psycho is able to transform into any known predatory animal, including man. His claws are much longer and sharper then the average demon, and senses are incredibly keen.

When Psycho enters combat, he will scout out his opponents and attack the one he feels is most vulnerable to his attacks. Psycho is not above performing surprise attacks, and enjoys foes who put up a good fight. He hates to kill outright, however, preferring to prolong the hunt for as long as possible before finally pouncing on his target. He avoids large battles whenever possible, and performs "hit-and-run" strikes. He charges out from somewhere in one form, strikes his target, changes to another form, and retreats for a while, then repeats the process.

Appearance: As a human, Psycho appears to be a dark young man with a feral gleam to his eyes. He has a rounded, grim visage, dark eyes, lank, dark hair, and a few broken teeth (funny how those breaks make the teeth look pointed...). He wears a leather jacket, blue jeans, tennis shoes, and nothing else. In his natural state, Psycho is five feet tall, and covered with short, black fur. Depending on his current needs, features from various predatory animals are obvious. He has been known to grow small, bat-like wings, a wolf's snout, cat's ears, etc. The features which remain constant, however, are Psycho's unnaturally long claws and teeth and his large, white eyes with no apparent pupils. Psycho typically reeks of spilled blood and death.

ENFORCER (ALZOL)

Val	Char	Cost	100+	Disadvantages
55*	STR	35	20	2x STUN from Magic
18	DEX	24	10	1½x STUN, BODY from Cold Iron
28	CON	36	25	Berserk In Battle, 8-, 8-
17*	BODY	10	20	Psych Lim: Fanatic loyalty to Forgotten Gods
13	INT	3		
20	EGO	20	15	Psych Lim: Killer
28	PRE	18	5	Distinctive Features: Radiates cold
2	COM	-4		
15	PD	6	25	Distinctive Features: Large skeletal figure
20	ED	14		
15	REC	0	10	Hunted by the Circle 8-
5	SPD	22	10	Hunted by DEMON 8-
56	END	2	20	Hunted by Police 14-
55*	STUN	1	161	Demon Bonus
			20	Overconfident
			10	2d6 Unluck
			15	1d6 STUN/Phase from Holy Items
			38	Additional Demon Bonus

*Chars From Growth Already Figured In

Cost	Power	END
25	1 ½d6 HKA (3d6 w/STR), Clawed Fingers	2(3)
23	1d6 RKA Damage Shield, Cold, 0 END	0
15	Damage Resistance (15 PD, 15 ED)	
20	75% rED Reduction vs. Cold Only (-2)	
30	50% rPD Reduction	
30	Full Life Support	
25	0 END on 50 STR	0
15	10 pts Growth, 0 END	0
25	Shapeshift to Any Humanoid Form, ½ END	1
10	1 BODY Regeneration	
5	+3 DCV (Mists, Skeletal form), Only in Normal Shape (-¼)	
8	FAM: Ancient Weapons (Missile, Melee, Etc.)	
3	Persuasion 15-	

If he regains his Scythe, add:

Cost	Power	END
20	Multipower (40 points), OAF-Scythe	
2 u	Desolidification, Affected by Holy Attacks	4
2 u	Invisibility vs. IR, UV, N-Ray	4
52	2d6 (4d6 w/STR) HKA, Affects physical world and Desolidified, OAF Scythe	10
7	3 Levels with Scythe	

OCV: 6; **DCV:** 6; **ECV:** 7; **Phases:** 3,5,8,10,12

Costs:	Chars		Powers		Total		Disadv		Base
	187	+	234	=	421	=	321	+	100

Background: The creature that calls itself Enforcer is actually Alzol, the only remaining representative of the once numerous Death Demons. The appearance of these Demons, and Enforcer in particular, is a possible basis for the myths of a "Grim Reaper." Centuries ago, a great war within the ranks of the Death Demons broke out, over which one was the most powerful. Enforcer, being quite cunning, decided against immediate involvement, and merely observed the others until their numbers had been reduced to a handful. These he easily dispatched, ending the dispute forever. The Wizard then approached him, seeking the aid of the Death Demons in the second attack on Earth. The Enforcer immediately accepted, and has fought at the side of The Wizard ever since, even though he lost his magic scythe during that failed campaign.

Distinctive Quote: <Evil grin>

(As the personality section, below, indicates, The Enforcer tends to be laconic.)

Personality: Enforcer is practical and cunning before a battle, but rarely thinks while fighting. Enforcer enjoys being strong, and loves power. He also respects The Wizard, as well as the Forgotten Gods, and hopes to gain more power from both when the latter are freed; it is only for this reason that he submits to the orders of The Wizard, and his tendency to take everything to extremes converts this loyalty and respect into seeming fanaticism. He rarely speaks, preferring to let his actions do his speaking for him.

His demeanor is grim.

Powers/Tactics: The Enforcer draws power directly from his home plane. His very essence drains the life of those who attempt to touch him. Being a death demon, the Enforcer is incredibly strong and tough. What's more, his skeletal body makes it hard to hit him as many weapons simply pass through the holes in his body. With his magical scythe, Enforcer also gains the ability to bend life around his body, and transform himself into a mere shadow.

The Enforcer likes to use Presence attacks in battle to immobilize foes so that he can more easily dispatch them. His preferred victims are those who are scrupulously good (heroes with one or more of the following psychological limitations, or similar ones: Code vs Killing, Protects Innocents, Honorable), or those who use magic. He likes to use either his bony hands or his scythe in battle. He flees if his foes strike exclusively from great ranges, but otherwise fights until ordered to quit or all foes are down.

Appearance: As a human, the Enforcer appears to be heavily muscled. He has light brown hair, ice-blue eyes, and stands just inches shorter than the average human male. In his normal demonic state, The Enforcer stands close to nine feet tall, and appears to be a human skeleton surrounded in mists and shrouded in a cloak seemingly composed entirely of shadow. A pale blue light radiates from his otherwise empty eye sockets, and the air around him is chillingly cold.

RUNT (MENNIGRASZ)

Val	Char	Cost	100+	Disadvantages
60*	STR	30	20	1 ½x STUN, Body from Magic
20	DEX	30	15	Delights in mass destruction
18	CON	16	15	"Yes-man"
16	BODY	12	25	Distinctive Features: Small, 4-armed monster
8	INT	-2		
20	EGO	20	10	Hunted by Demon 8-
10	PRE	0	10	Hunted by the Circle 8-
4	COM	-3	20	Hunted by Police 14-
12*	PD	0	135	Demon Bonus
12*	ED	4		
6	SPD	30		
12	REC	0		
50	END	2		
45	STUN	0		

*Chars From DI Already Figured In

Cost	Power	END
25	1 ½d6 HKA (3d6 w/STR), Claws	2(3)
27	4 Levels Density Increase, Always On, 0 END, Persistent	0
13	1 Level Shrinking, Always On, 0 END, Persistent	0
5	Extra Limbs: Two additional arms	
24	(8,8) Armor	
15	Mindlink with the Wizard, Any Distance, Any Dimension	1
25	Shapeshift to any humanoid form, ½ END	1
10	1 BODY Regeneration	
24	Life Support: Self Contained Breathing, No Need to Eat or Excrete, Doesn't Age, Immune to Intense Pressure & Extreme temperatures.	
15	½ END on STR	3
3	Climbing 13-	
25	+5 Levels in Hand-to-Hand Combat	

OCV: 7; **DCV:** 9; **ECV:** 7; **Phases:** 2,4,6,8,10,12

Costs:	Chars		Powers		Total		Disadv		Base
	139	+	211	=	350	=	250	+	100

Background: For every demon who possesses power, there are millions more who are powerless, dejected and enslaved. They exist for no other reason than to to serve the demonic lord who created them. Few of these creatures ever amount to more than wretched slaves.

The lucky members of this drone class are the Demon lords' personal servants. While these creatures are still bullied and picked on, their living conditions are still vastly superior to those of their kindred.

Runt has, and always shall be, one of those creatures. He was originally created by the Demon Prince Tchal Aka, but was later endeared to Morgalis when he slew Tchal Aka in personal combat. Since then, Runt has always been by Morgalis' side. He knows it is his destiny to serve and has no desire to do anything else.

Distinctive Quote: "Yes, master... Yessssss."

Personality: Runt is the ultimate "yes-man," preferring to praise the thoughts of Morgalis than to think for himself. Most of the time, his dialogue contains a lot of "yes"es, praise for his "Master," etc. He should be an annoyance to both sides. Runt also delights in mass destruction — the more mindless — the better. Note, however, that he is not stupid; he is merely too lazy to think for himself.

Powers/Tactics: Runt, a small, dense creature, is only half the size of a full grown man, though he possesses a mass somewhat greater than that of a normal man. This increased mass enhances his strength to truly superhuman levels, and also increases his recuperative abilities. As a result, he is able to employ his full strength with less effort than it would take for another being to do so, and he recovers from most injuries at a fantastic rate. He also possesses two additional arms, making him an excellent hand-to-hand (to-hand) combatant.

Runt frequently performs grab maneuvers on heroes, so that he can hurl them at cars, buildings, public monuments, or (as a last resort) other foes. Runt prefers using maneuvers that will cause as much destruction as possible.

Appearance: In his natural state, Runt appears to be a three foot tall gorilla with an unnaturally large mouth and four huge, powerful arms. His fur is a dark black in color; He has unnaturally large, pool-like eyes. As the human called Runt, Mennigrasz appears to be short and fat, wears an English Touring cap, a light green tweed suit, and brown and gray saddle Oxfords.

STREET GANGS

TYPICAL STREET GANG MEMBER

Val	Char	Cost	0+	Disadvantages
11	STR	1	15	Follows Gang's Code
11	DEX	3	10	Distinctive Features: Colors
11	CON	2	5	Reputation: Gang's Reputation, 8-
10	BODY	0		
10	INT	0		
9	EGO	-2		
10	PRE	0		
10	COM	0		
5	PD	3		
3	ED	1		
2	SPD	-1		
4	REC	0		
22	END	0		
22	STUN	0		

Cost	Skill	END
12	Dirty Infighting	
	Maneuver / **OCV** / **DCV** / **Damage/Effect**	
	Punch +0 +2 4d6	
	Low Blow -1 +1 2d6 NND	
	Kidney Blow -2 0 ½d6 HKA	
3	Streetwise 11-	
2	AK: Gang Turf 11-	
2	Fam. w/Street Weaponry (Chains, Baseball bats, etc.)	
2	Random PS (usually a Hobby or Interest) 11-	
2	+1" Running	1

OCV: 3; **DCV:** 3; **ECV:** 3; **Phases:** 6,12

Costs:	Chars		Powers		Total		Disadv		Base
	7	+	23	=	30	=	30	+	0

Background: This represents a stylized comic-book street thug. A few brief write-ups of specific gangs follow the template for a gang leader, below. The stats above reflect the typical male "street punk." For exceptional or female street kids, the GM may adapt these stats as he/she sees fit.

If the true nature of the Demons is revealed in the presence of a gang member, the GM may roll on the following chart for each street kid present (1d6):

1 Turns against the Demons
2 Flees in horror, quits street gang life forever.
3.-5 Assumes that this is a trick played by the PCs, and ignores situation.
6 Kid thinks that this is great, becomes fanatical follower of the Demons, may even ask to host one or learn to use magic.

Some sample gangs, with their preferred weapon sets, follow the description of a "typical" Gang Leader.

TYPICAL GANG LEADER

Val	Char	Cost	50+	Disadvantages
13	STR	3	15	Follows Gang's Code
14	DEX	12	10	Distinctive Features: Colors
11	CON	2		
11	BODY	2		
11	INT	1		
10	EGO	0		
13	PRE	3		
10	COM	0		
5	PD	2		
2	ED	0		
3	SPD	6		
5	REC	0		
22	END	0		
25	STUN	1		

Cost	Skills	END
21	Street Fighting	
	Maneuver / **OCV** / **DCV** / **Damage/Effect**	
	Punch +0 +2 4d6 Normal	
	Roundhouse -2 +1 6d6 Normal	
	Low Blow -1 +1 2d6 NND	
	Kidney Blow -2 +0 1d6+1 HKA	
	Disarm -1 +1 Disarm at 23 STR	
4	+3 PD/3 ED Nonresistent, OIF Leather Jacket	
3	Streetwise 12-	
3	Any One Skill (Normally Oratory or Persuasion)	
2	AK: Gang Turf 11-	
2	FAM: Street Weaponry (Chains, Baseball Bats)	
1	Tactics 8-	
2	PS or KS: Hobby or Area of Interest 11-	

OCV: 3; **DCV:** 3; **ECV:** 3; **Phase:** 4,8,12

Costs:	Chars		Powers		Total		Disadv		Base
	32	+	43	=	75	=	25	+	50

Background: This is intended to represent the person who has "earned" a leadership position in a gang by strength, determination, and cunning. Many gang leaders would have higher INT scores, more skills, and a few Psychological Limitations. A (very) few even have some points of experience spent, as well.

One important detail to remember when using street characters in combat: many of these individuals may refuse to fight fairly, and will take any advantages that they can to win a fight, or to escape if losing.

SAMPLE GANGS

THE SHARKS

The Sharks are a bunch of dissatisfied youths who are sick and tired of the edicts of their parents. All members wear gray clothing, and employ either chains (Add +3d6 to STR, and 1" Stretching, with a 2d6 BODY 2 DEF Entanglement on a 14-) or Blackjacks (+2d6 HA, No KB). Several members also possess non-combat skills (Lockpicking, Stealth, etc.). Their leader, Albert Dinnesen (usually called "Fin") has a martial arts style based on the Chain (instead of Dirty Infighting, he has Martial Block, Martial Strike (Total Damage: 7d6 + 1), Martial Throw (6d6 + v/5 + 1), and Martial Disarm (Disarm at STR 43).

THE JETTS

This gang is predominantly Hispanic, and is unusual as it has a few female members (most street gangs are exclusively male). The Jetts were formed to protect their neighborhood from "outside influences", but don't mind hitting up local businesses for a little protection money. Members wear black or dark brown jackets, usually leather, often stolen. Membership mixed between Brawlers (knife armed, with one level in combat and a blunt weapon of some sort), Thugs (increase stats as: STR 15, CON 13, PD 8, ED 3, REC 6, END 26, STUN 25), and Street Fighters (kids with Dirty Infighting). The leader, Enrico Estevez, is a "typical" leader.

THE STUDS

The Studs were originally just a group of friends that hung out together, but they have since become a large gang, known for their violent crimes. This gang consists primarily of Thugs (increase stats as: STR 15, CON 13, PD 8, ED 3, REC 6, END 26, STUN 25), with a few pistol-wielding (.38 Special; 1d6 RKA, 6 charges) members. All members wear leather jackets, and after each fight they win, each member affixes a metal stud to his jacket. The current leader is the member with the most studs. Most also carry knives (½d6 HKA).

THE RENEGADES

The Renegades is more of a home for runaways than anything else. They commit crimes simply to survive. They specialize in shoplifting, picking pockets and street hustles. Members of this gang habitually wear brown jackets (often of leather), and red bandanas tied around either an arm or a leg. Their leader, "Stick" (he uses his real name so rarely that he's forgotten it) does not wear padded clothing, but he does use a pair of batons (+2d6 HA) in combat, hence his nickname.

THE PREDATORS

This is a group of paramilitary skinheads. They are known for their racist edicts and fascist organization. This gang dresses primarily in red or orange, and often uses commando-style "war paint" prior to a fight. All members carry knives, and several also have pistols (as per the Studs, above). Their leader has Distinctive Features (his nose has been broken at least five times, and he has a large scar on one cheek), carries a large (1d6 +1) Bowie knife, and hates almost everyone who is not a member of his gang.

THE ANGELS

One of the city's few all-female gangs, the Angels are more of a social clique then they are a gang. All members wear white jackets with the word "Angels" written in gold thread on the back. In combat, they either use an assortment of Dirty Infighting maneuvers (select as desired), or blackjacks (+2d6 HA, STUN only, no KB). Their leader, Vanessa, is described in the "Angels in Heaven" episode, above.

THE ROCKERS

This is the only other mixed gender gang in the city. The members are heavily influenced by the Rockers of 1960's England, although they also listen to modern "punk" music. They are a hodgepodge of individuals who simply act alike. No two Rockers ever dress alike, however, as each wears an individualized wardrobe, make-up, hair color, and style designed primarily to shock onlookers. If they had a leader before the Wizard showed up, they were never aware of it. Any common weapons or fighting styles are possible.

THE HAWKS

This gang is primarily composed of wealthy brats rebelling against their parents. They tend to be the smallest but best-armed and best dressed gang on the streets. All members wear jackets with a large "Hawk" logo on the back, and mirrored sunglasses.

THE BACK STREET BRAWLERS

This is probably the largest single gang in the City. All wear denim jackets with the gang name burned onto the back. The leader of the Brawlers is Jerry Mitchell, a kid with a high PRE and a strong desire to get into big business. Since his family can't afford to put him there legally, he has decided to find another route. All members are proficient at Dirty Infighting, and a few have weapons as well.

From these basic outlines, other similar gangs should be easily designed by the GM, if needed.

OPTIONAL NPC VILLAIN

(OUR MAN FROM DEMON)

LORD THORNE
(SIR HENRY WILLIAM THORNESBY III)

15 STR	18 DEX	2 CON	12 BODY	33 INT
29 EGO	30 PRE	16 COM	5 PD	5 ED
6 SPD	8 REC	56 END	35 STUN	

Powers, Talents and Skills: 120 pt. Mystic Power Pool; EC: Invulnerability, IIF: Ring of Okarith [Grants: 15 Pt Power Defense, Hardened; 21 Pt. Mental Defense, Hardened; 2 BODY Regeneration; Armor (+10 PD, 10 ED); Full Life Support; and ½ Resistant Damage Reduction vs PD & ED]; Danger Sense, 14, Cannot be surprised, Mystic Powers 16-; Scientist (History 18, Astronomy 14-, Parapsychology 14-, Psychology 13-); Scholar (Literature 12-, Occult Studies 14-, World Religions 14-); Acting 15-; Bribery 15-; Bureaucratics 15-; Conversation 15-; Seduction 15-; High Society 15-; Oratory 15-; Persuasion 15-; Sleight of Hand 13-; Tactics 16-; Traveler; Well-Connected; +1 Overall Level.

100+ Disadvantages: 1 ½x STUN — Magic; Wants to rule the world; Considers all other beings merely tools for his use; Wants to live forever; Casts no reflection; 2d6 STUN/Phase from contact with pure silver; Reputation 11-, Very Dangerous/Evil person; Hunted by the Circle 8-; Hunted by Doctor Destroyer 11; Hunted by major Demon and its minions, 11-; Rival: Professor Clinton Avery (Professional); Secret ID (Sir Henry William Thornesby III); Experience.

Background: Thorne was one of the guiding forces behind the formation of DEMON, and has been one of its key figures ever since (some even feel that he is the leader of DEMON!).

He possesses a vast array of magic items and almost limitless mystic knowledge, which makes him one of the most feared men alive. Long ago, he stole some of the Essence of an entity called Xortec, one of the Forgotten Gods. This greatly increased his power, but it also rendered him vulnerable to magic and silver, cost him his reflection, and earned him that entity's enmity forever.

Notes: Thorne is a vicious, evil, self-serving man. His involvement (if, indeed he is involved) is due mainly to his desire to obtain both the three artifacts and possibly the services of these Demons at a later date. If a few superheroes die in the process, all the better! At least he will be able to get what he wants...

HEROES ASSEMBLE!

We want to hear from you. Please take a minute to photocopy this page (or tear it out), answer the questions and mail it to us. We're trying to make *Champions*™ the best it can be, so we need your feedback. When you speak, we listen.

1. Why did you buy *Demons Rule*™? ______________________________

2. What did you like best about *Demons Rule?* ______________________________

3. What did you like least about *Demons Rule?* ______________________________

4. How did you hear about *Demons Rule?* ______________________________

5. Which do you prefer, scenarios or sourcebooks? ______________________________

6. Are you willing to pay for better covers? Which ones have been your favorite? ______________________________

7. What other role-playing games do you play? ______________________________

8. What other products would you most like to see from HERO games? ______________________________

9. If you don't mind, please state:

   your age: _____years
   your sex: _____male _____ female
   where you bought this book:__________________________

Thanks! That wasn't so hard for a Hero, was it? Now complete the blank below, photocopy it, and mail it to: HERO Games, c/o ICE, PO Box 1605, Charlottesville, VA 22902.

Name:______________________________
Street Address:______________________________
City, State:______________________ **Zip:**__________